A Deathful Ridge

A Deathful Ridge

A Novel of Everest

by
J.A. Wainwright

Mosaic Press
Oakville, ON. - Buffalo, N.Y.

Canadian Cataloguing in Publication Data

Wainwright, J.A., 1946-
A deathful ridge

ISBN 0-88962-633-2 HC   ISBN 0-88962-650-2 PB
I. Title.
PS8595.A54D42 1997   C813'.54   C97-930017-7
PR9199.3.W34D42 1997

Published by MOSAIC PRESS, P.O. Box 1032, Oakville, Ontario, L6J 5E9, Canada. Offices and warehouse at 1252 Speers Road, Units #1&2, Oakville, Ontario, L6L 5N9, Canada and Mosaic Press, 85 River Rock Drive, Suite 202, Buffalo, N.Y., 14207, USA.

MOSAIC PRESS, in Canada:
1252 Speers Road, Units #1&2,
Oakville, Ontario, L6L 5N9
Phone / Fax: (905) 825-2130
E-mail:
cp507@freenet.toronto.on.ca

MOSAIC PRESS, in the USA:
85 River Rock Drive, Suite 202,
Buffalo, N.Y., 14207
Phone / Fax: 1-800-387-8992
E-mail:
cp507@freenet.toronto.on.ca

MOSAIC PRESS in the UK and Europe:
DRAKE INTERNATIONAL SERVICES
Market House, Market Place,
Deddington, Oxford. OX15 OSF

Mosaic Press acknowledges the assistance of the Canada Council, the Ontario Arts Council and the Dept. of Canadian Heritage, Government of Canada, for their support of our publishing programme.

Copyright © J.A. Wainwright, 1997
ISBN 0-88962-633-2
Cover photograph by: Frank Nugent
Cover and book design by: Susan Parker
Printed and bound in Canada

for Marjorie and Christopher

And how my feet recross'd the deathful ridge
No memory in me lives.

Tennyson, *The Holy Grail*

Great climbers have been caught -- I admit it.

George Mallory

ACKNOWLEDGEMENTS

Many of the facts and some of the speculations in this novel about George Mallory and his climbs on Everest can be found in the books listed below, along with much of the information about mountains and climbing, especially in regard to Snowdon and Everest.

David Pye, *George Leigh Mallory*
(London: Oxford University Press, 1927)

James Ramsay Ullman, *Kingdom of Adventure: Everest*
(New York: William Sloane, 1947)

David Robertson, *George Mallory*
(London: Faber and Faber, 1969)

Francis Keenlyside, *Peaks and Pioneers:
The Story of Mountaineering*
(London: Paul Elek, 1975)

Chris Bonington, *The Everest Years: A Climber's Life*
(London: Hodder and Stoughton, 1986)

Tom Holzel & Audrey Salkeld, *First on Everest:
The Mystery of Mallory & Irvine*
(New York: Henry Holt, 1986)

Lorna Siggins, *Everest Calling; Ascent of the Dark Side:
The Mallory-Irvine Ridge*
(London: Mainstream Publishing, 1994)

Captain John Noel's film *The Epic of Everest* is housed in the National Film Institute and Television Archives in London.

I am grateful to Timothy Findley for his permission to quote from *The Wars* and to use part of his story of Robert Ross.

The lines from Bob Dylan's "Idiot Wind" are used with the permission of Geoff Rusen, Ram's Horn Music (1975).

Thanks to: Peter, Carol Ann, and Kate for the farm in Colombeix (*la France profonde*); my uncle and aunt, John and Althea Storr, for all those early books on Everest; Chris and Jane for introducing me to Wales; Edgar and Irving for waiting patiently; Philip for all the climbs; and Marlene for keeping the faith. Thanks, as well, to Peggy, Barbara, Mike, Eleanor, Margaret, Stirling, Rich, and Malcolm for listening to the plans before they were fulfilled; and Yianni who will never read this story, but knows it anyway.

ONE

When I awake in the tent there is a man beside me. For some reason I don't question the tent, the extreme cold, the wind that is howling outside. It is the man who holds me. The face is familiar. It is a face from books. I am afraid to begin this, afraid of the ascent and descent. More writers are killed on the way down than on the way up. "You're Mallory," I say.

George Leigh Mallory (1886-1924), born Mobberley, Cheshire, educated Winchester School and Cambridge. Climbed in Wales and Swiss Alps (on summit of Mount Blanc at 18). Taught at Charterhouse School (among students, Robert Graves). Friend of Rupert Brooke, Lytton Strachey, and Virginia Woolf. Served with the Royal Garrison Artillery in France during W.W.I. Three Everest expeditions (1921, 1922, 1924). Last sighted on Everest by Noel Odell "going strong for the top" with Andrew (Sandy) Irvine, June 8, 1924. Galahad after the Grail to those who knew him. When asked by American reporters why he wanted to climb the world's highest mountain he replied, "Because it's there." Though even his friends didn't agree on what he meant by this.

The terrain beneath the Northeast Ridge of Everest consists of giant slabs of rock tilted at impossible angles. Bare and windswept they are difficult enough to negotiate, but covered with new

1

snow, granular and unconsolidated, they are deadly adversaries. Imagine traversing them with the lower half of your body covered entirely, your feet sliding out from underneath you at every step, the ice-axe useless in your hand, the force of the jet stream around you like an explosion without end. "Blasted on the face of Everest," someone said.

On June 4, 1924, after reaching 28,128 feet, higher than any man before him, Edward Norton was descending alone. He kept turning around to check on a companion he was sure was there. Who is that other who climbs behind you? Once, in the Great Couloir, he could not force his body to take a step across a narrow gap, a movement he had made hundreds of times before. Trembling, he stood on the brink. Then he took his companion's hand. Almost immediately above him was the summit. Chomolungma: Goddess Mother of the World.

The archivist and I go down to the basement of the British Alpine Club. When I first look up the address in *London A-Z*, I read it as Charlotte Street, W.I, a more prestigious location than where I eventually end up, at Charlotte Road near the Old Street Tube Station in the East End. The reading room is tiny, like a tent at altitude, and the bookshelves lean like cornices over a neophyte climber. But there is a solidity to Mr. Peters, the archivist, who has promised me a look at the original of the note Mallory left at Camp VI for Odell:

Things aren't too neat and tidy here. The stove is somewhere below on the Rongbuk Glacier. Sandy and I cooperated in that! We hope to see you at IV tomorrow, and we can all go down together. I'm sure we'll have enough oxygen for the final push, but the cylinders are a beastly weight. The weather is with us!

Mallory had a reputation for absent-mindedness and even carelessness when it came to his secondary climbing gear. Apparently he left a torch and lantern behind at VI, items which might have proved useful had he wished to signal his whereabouts to

2

those lower down as night fell. So it is more than ironic that the letter itself is not in the Alpine Club safe where it is supposed to be, nor among other papers which Mr. Peters shuffles through with some optimism.

"Ah, here is a copy," he says happily. And so it is, contained in a dusty black and white frame. I recognize the crevasse between my romantic aspirations and the reality I am grasping. This is a reproduction sealed off by glass and wood. Following Mr. Peters down those basement stairs, I was sure I would soon be holding a piece of paper in my hands that Mallory had held, that had been exposed to the winds of Everest at 27,000 feet, and that would bind me to the man and mountain like a fixed rope. It is not a piece of paper I have been seeking, but an icon that no longer exists. "It hung for years on the wall of the Royal Geographical Society," says Mr. Peters, and I am not sure whether he is referring to this copy or to the vanished original. Then, with his back to me, already turning away towards the stairs, he asks, "Have you seen the sciax?" At least that's what I hear. And in my disappointment over the letter, I don't seek a translation.

"I think it's here somewhere," he says, diving into what looks to be a hanging pile of axe-handles, ringing them madly like wooden chimes as his hands scrabble amongst them. And then it hits me between the eyes: the ice-axe, the one found by the 1933 Team lying on exposed slabs at almost 28,000 feet. At first it was thought to be Mallory's, but later the three cut grooves in the handle below the head were determined to be Irvine's mark. Great speculation followed the discovery. Had it fallen to this spot or been laid down by a weary climber? Or had the climber let go of it when he had fallen? Had the axe been to the summit of the world, or was it a sad instrument of defeat that could not save its owner, no matter what its maker, Willisch of Tasch in the Zermatt Valley, had intended? All archival questions now, it seems.

"This it it, I think," announces Mr. Peters, and turns in a wide arc with the flat blade carving the air between us. I take it from him, a surprisingly hefty combination of wood and iron, so much heavier than the molybdenum steel axes of today, and as he wanders off in further search of the letter, I swing it, one-handed, between the icy shelves and cabinets I will never climb, and run my fingers over the parallel grooves, feeling something, a presence, an absence I cannot define. Mallory, whom I am chasing, probably held this while Irvine checked the troublesome oxygen equipment or secured the rope between them at the base of the First Step. And the many palms and fingers that have burnished the handle in the sixty-two years since it was found cannot erase his touch. I want-- no, I covet-- this axe, as I have never coveted any material object in my life. Mr. Peters wouldn't notice, would he, if I quietly slipped it inside my leather jacket (too short!) and then told him I had returned it to the collection. Or what if I returned in the dark--eyes scanning the metal-barred windows for entry possibilities--or hid in the loo overnight, or I could crack his skull and run with the axe to my own private slopes of isolation.

"It should be behind glass," I tell him when he comes back." In the RGS along with the letter, so people like me can only watch from a distance (like Odell when Mallory and Irvine 'stepped into legend')? I hand back the axe, and watch him toss it casually into the swinging pile. In some ways, it is as close as I will get.

This happens before I go up on the mountain myself. Among other things behind my desire to do so is the question of heroism, how what Mallory did and tried to do were perceived in his world.

In 1909, shortly after meeting George, who is twenty-three, and climbing with him in Wales, Geoffrey Winthrop Young writes a poem. Here is the last verse: "Companions at the close, on a windy ridge/Where knights alone must venture./Those who climb and lift the veil/Will grasp the glory/Know the Grail." The key to the Galahad club is that the Grail is attainable for those who climb to the final precipice and step *through* not *off*. Merely stepping off results in what some have called the Icarus Syndrome, in which Mallory becomes just one more dead climber.

In July, 1924, only a month after Mallory lifts the veil, Geoffrey Young provides an obituary paean for the British public: "Chivalry and youth--these and the fiery spirit that burned within them to the end bore them higher than Everest itself." "Youth"? Irvine, maybe. He is only twenty-two; but Mallory is ten days short of his thirty-eighth birthday when he *disappears*. And one profound reason Young can write like this, can deny the Icarus Syndrome, is because there are no bodies. Remember Breughel's painting, the boy's legs sticking out of the ocean? Real boy. Real ocean. Real failure.

Let's go back to Odell for a moment. He's down at 26,000 feet, a support climber who's supposed to prepare Camp VI for the descent from the summit. He's waiting around for the weather to lift and climbs a crag. Suddenly everything clears up above, and he sees Mallory and Irvine momentarily on the rock formation known as the Second Step, some two thousand feet higher, before the cloud cover (read *veil*) sets in. The point is, their wings are still intact, the wax hasn't melted, no one sees the fall, hears the cries (they are probably higher than Icarus since his combination of feathers and wax couldn't get five miles high, whatever that story would have us believe).

I say, "one profound reason Young can write like this..." but I'm not really convinced. In Italy Young had already seen all the dead bodies he could ever imagine, as had Mallory on the Western Front. In fact Young's climbing career would never be the same from the time he lost his left leg above the knee in August 1917, serving in the Ambulance Unit near another knight-errant, Ernest Hemingway, who said that words like *grail* and *chivalry* sounded hollow after his own knee-wound.

The photo is originally black and white, but has been coloured by the photographer, Captain John Noel. Mallory is the odd man out. The rest are in some recognizable form of cold-weather gear--heavy jackets or vests, scarves, gloves; all of them are wearing hats of fur or wool. Geoffrey Bruce sports a fedora. Irvine looks like a twenties version of an outdoors fashion model with his open smile and matching jacket, pants, and puttees. The jacket has zippers on chest pockets that may or may not be functional. His hat is straight from the Tilley catalogue. Seven of the nine men in the picture are in a standard pose. Standing in the back row, Norton, Odell, and Wheeler have their hands clasped behind their backs.

Sitting in the front, Shebbeare, Bruce, Somervell, and Hazard rest their elbows on their knees above crossed ankles and bring their hands together. Irvine is also standing but has his hands in his pockets, perhaps casually, perhaps because he does not know what else to do with them. His open grin suggests that he has not fully measured the mountain. The others have mouths that curve politely, as if Noel has just said, "Gentlemen, please."

Mallory is in the back row, dressed in a brown wool suit with a white dress shirt (the collar looks pressed) underneath. He has no hat, so his hair, close-cropped at the sides (revealing slightly protruding ears) and a longer thatch on top, is visible. His body language is palpable. His hands are on his hips, gunslinger fashion, with his fingers resting slightly inside his pockets; his right finnesko or Norwegian camp boot is set on the left shoulder of Shebbeare; his mouth is a straight line of irony and aggression (though the climbing brotherhood would call it determination). While the others are still, or recede from the camera eye, Mallory's eyes challenge the camera. He threatens the stability of the frame and the comfort of the viewer who wants only to say, "They're all dead now. This is the past." Captain Noel knows something, though, as he looks through the pinhole, waiting for the shutter to click: "He was possessed by Everest, and pictured himself on the summit. It consumed him."

The sherpas were "coolies," usually referred to in the same breath as the donkeys that carried the supplies to Base Camp. In 1922, on the second expedition to Everest, they were more commonly known as "porters," but when seven of them died in an avalanche, Mallory wrote to his wife, Ruth, "They are so childlike, and seemingly unaware of the perils we face." Geoffrey Young wrote to Mallory about the accident, referring directly to the relationship between officers and men and, implicitly, between war and mountaineering: "On Everest you were with them every step of the way. Remember, in the war there were times we gave orders to our men and sent them to places we did not go."

Then there was the Yeti or Sukpa. The sherpas believed in its existence, and there were some unexplainable tracks, but, after all, civilized, rational men could not let their minds or time be taken up with such things. "They are child-like where questions of faith are concerned"? Who knows? But make no mistake, for the sherpas the Yeti was a figure of faith in the unknown, the inexplicable. It was something those who believed in the need for conclusions could never understand. The Yeti may even yet be a coolie in the mountains of the Western mind, but in the Himalayas, for those who live there rather than merely climb the slopes, such a being cannot be colonized.

In 1924 Major O.E. or E.O. Wheeler from Canada (the books, even the most recent ones, never say from exactly where) is a member of the expedition as a surveyor and support climber (did he get his expertise just in the Rockies or in all that rugged northern wilderness in general?). George tells Ruth: "You know how I feel about Canadians. I shall have to take a deep breath before I can admit to any friendship. God give me the oxygen!" That's fairly strong stuff, though the biographers don't provide any speculation on this bias. Mallory visited Canada in 1923 while on tour in North America to drum up support for the next year's summit bid. A Toronto lecture was cancelled (his Uncle Wilfred lived there), so instead he spent two days skiing in the Laurentians: "On sunny days a Canadian winter can be quite enjoyable, but even then the cold is penetrating." *Cold?* This from someone who'd bivouaced on Mt. Blanc during blizzards and been twice to Everest! You can see how far below zero the colony lies. A Canadian nanny, then, lurking in the background, too unimportant for the biographies?. Or were there some cowardly Canucks stationed near Mallory at Armentières? What's he going to do with me at 28,000 feet when I'm on the other end of our rope of words? These are questions I need to carry with me, as well as the books I've read. In dreams at altitude it's not the food that sustains you.

A bright, clear day on the west coast of England, 1895. The Mallory family is on holiday:
"George Mallory!" His mother calling.

The rock rises out of the sand, exposed at low tide on a stretch of beach away from the crowds. He climbs it because it's there. In his school blazer. His sisters and brother are watching. Their mother does not call them. She does not have to. I hear her cry, anxious, knowing what he can do. And my own voice.

"Okay, we're here. Now what?"

He looks at me with his nine-year old eyes. I am no bigger than he is, but I have a sense this is only the beginning. The water rolls in, cold Irish Sea water.

"We wait." And we do, until it covers our shoes and socks. I want to yell out. There are fishermen down the shore. "No," he says.

His mother is on the beach now, pleading with the fishermen. They arrive in their dinghy just as the tide turns, leaving its mark at mid-calf. "Sometimes," he says, "life is like a dream."

In August 1978, at the age of thirty-two, I have my first view of Mt. Blanc. I am on the road from Chamonix, looking across a valley at the Brenva Glacier. I take black and white photos with my Pentax, using a telescopic lens. When they are developed later, the glacier hangs over the valley like a tidal wave of frozen menace. The mountain on all sides of the ice and above it is huge, a full three thousand feet higher than Mt. Robson, the highest peak in the Canadian Rockies, yet only slightly more than half the height of Everest. I am not thinking of Mallory at all. It is too early for him. I am thinking instead of a trip to Leeds a dozen years previously when my mother's elderly cousin, a very intelligent but very proper woman who disapproves of every inch of my Canadian frame and sixties attitude, tells me about Addle Crag as I am leaving her house for a morning walk. The crag is, I take it, a local hill of some steepness and renown, and will be for me, she implies with an empirical smile, a test. I want to rise to the occasion, but end up on my back in a field, staring at the sun through toke-filtered eyes. When I return for lunch a few hours later, she inquires about my ascent. "Ah, well," I reply. "I got sidetracked." Ignoring my colloquial evasion, which probably cannot be translated into the Queen's English, she asks me the question which will haunt my young manhood, try as I might to dismiss her as a repressed, old spinster: "Do you ever climb mountains?"

Mallory climbed Mount Blanc at eighteen on his first trip to the Alps. There is no evidence that he had previously done anything other than shinny up the drainpipes of his parents' house and walk the rooflines. Though there is a story that at seven, scolded for misbehaving, he climbed to the roof of the church where his father (and his father before him) was rector. But no visits to North Wales yet, no cliffs, or icy chimneys, or routes that would bear his name.

In 1904, R.L.G. Irving, the College Tutor at Winchester, where Mallory was studying mathematics, chose him with another student for an Alpine climbing holiday. Why? Perhaps part of the answer lies in the homoerotic attraction that Graham Irving, like so many Englishmen of his generation, unconsciously revealed: "Mallory was strong and lithe, but of a moderate build....until his early thirties his skin was completely unlined. He was very handsome, though his natural good looks were so much more gentle than rugged, and he moved with a female grace that belied the power of his very *male* accomplishments. Those who loved him did so for all his traits." None of the pictures I have seen of Mallory suggest this kind of aesthetic precision, but I have to admit that the *talk* about his features is compelling, even if Lytton Strachey, who consciously revealed all, crosses over to the absurd (the very term he used to describe mountains) side of decadence in 1909: "He's the exact height of Christ, with the body of Michelangelo's David, and a mien--my heart flutters!-- of such elegance and beauty that I weep for what will be lost should he ever fall." He is writing to Clive and Vanessa Bell and proclaims that "Only Virginia will know whereof I speak." Is her walk into the water thirty-two years later a stepping *through* as well?

It is my first time at altitude, too. I'm sick, but so is he. We are in the Vellot hut for the night with Graham Irving. The floor is a sheet of ice, and snow is sifting in through the wall cracks and around the windows. I can't believe how cold it is, nor what we are wearing. Like them, I have on three sweaters (the top one of heavy wool) and an anorak, two pairs of pants (corduroy on the outside), three pairs of socks inside what look like regular hiking boots with crampons attached, thick mittens, and a canvas hat with a wide brim that can obviously be tied down over my ears. It's not enough. We have brought some bread and cheese, and boil some snow on the tiny stove for tea. There are rugs to serve as sleeping bags. Today we traversed across an ice slope, held together by about twenty feet of rope tied to special belts around our waists. It was like a recurring dream I had as a child. I would climb, against my will, to the top of a tall tower. When I emerged on the parapet it was slanting downward, and I would invariably slide toward the edge, never quite falling over, but always anticipating the plunge with terror. I want to talk to him about this, but I'm still trying to figure out the rules. He's only eighteen, not yet at Cambridge. He looks at me. There will be no rules on Everest. I listen.

"Dr. Paccard and his porter, Balmat, did this in two days in 1787, George. They had alpenstocks and nails in their shoes."

"What time of year was it?" *Mallory, I know, hasn't read any of the mountaineering books in the Winchester library.*

"August, two weeks before us. It was cold, about -20 degrees F. The doctor's right hand froze, and it was days before the feeling came back to the fingers. He was also snow-blind for several hours after the descent."

"What good were the alpenstocks? Wouldn't they just have hindered them?"

"On the contrary. If they fell into shallow, snow-filled crevasses, they held the stocks horizontally across the gap and were able to climb out. When they came to open crevasses, they would lay their implements across them and crawl over on their hands and knees."

"Was there any proof they made the summit? After all, they hadn't a camera."

"Oh, yes, the doctor tied a red handkerchief to a stick. Those watching from below could see it through a telescope."

Mallory sits back against a wall. The handkerchief on a stick is so simple, so understated. It seems to bother him. "Why not a flag?"

"Which flag, dear chap? They didn't climb for France. I doubt the king even knew at the time, though he certainly would have heard about it afterwards. They did it for themselves. There are those who call Paccard the father of mountaineering."

"How did he die?"

"I don't know. Not on the mountain."

In the morning, the wind is terrible. It whips through the sweaters and the anorak as we climb the Bosses du Dromadaire towards the top. My headache is gone, but I am shaking with the cold. Since I am third, I do not have to cut any ice-steps, but that exertion might warm me a little. I can hear my heart thudding as I move upward through clouds of my own breath. There is no time to look down or around as we push the tops of our skulls into the wind. The rope is an umbilical cord that must not be severed. Suddenly I hear voices. Six men are descending. Four are rescuers who tell us that the other two have been trapped on the summit for four days by the near-blizzard conditions.

"Le vent," they say, "c'est une salope!" We keep going. Those on the telescopes below cannot imagine what it's like.

Later, Mallory will write: "Only those who have made the climb can understand the feelings of exultation and delight." How does the wind as bitch figure in this? Or does it at all? I am tired. My face feels as if it is cracking open and my hands are numb. The pace seems murderous, though each ice-step is several minutes in the making. Suddenly, as the sun breaks through, one of us seems to slip and we are jerked from our footing. We slide, building up speed, but Irving, who has been leading, hits out with his axe at the last step and we bounce hard against the rock outcrop beneath.

"Alright?" Irving asks.

"No damage done," says Mallory, and we ascend again.

Thirty minutes later, we are there, 15,771 feet. It's clear now, and Chamonix is aeons below. We can see the rescue party near the hut.

"Well done," Irving proclaims. I feel included, but they are both gazing out and up, as if another summit is looming, something commensurate with their vision of what this is about, beyond the peak

the gentle doctor climbed that now has an observatory with a protective south wall for weary travellers.

"The handkerchief," I say, but Mallory shakes his head and smiles. We leave nothing to mark our passage.

In October 1905, Mallory went up to Magdalene College, Cambridge. Three years later he acted in a production of *Comus* in celebration of the Milton Tercentenary. Rupert Brooke was the Attendant Spirit, and two granddaughters of Charles Darwin, Frances and Gwen, were stage assistants. Mallory was already friends with Darwin's grandson. In 1986 I visit Cambridge and sit in Magdalene's great dining hall, trying to gain a small sense of what it must have been like to have been an undergraduate in communal rooms like this one. The problem is I am alone in a space that is meant to hold three hundred. I lean on the long oak table and stare at the river. An antidote to loneliness in Mallory's day was the "Cambridge School of Friendship." A young *female* mountaineer, Cottie Saunders, wrote this about her observations of Mallory's circle:

> *Their closeness was unique....they loved one another and wanted to comprehend the nature of that love...to bring themselves closer together....It was a new way of doing things, a new voicing of feelings and ideas which was nothing short of amazing. No matter how problematical or disturbing the issue, they would speak it aloud.*

But the problematical and disturbing weren't usually approached as directly as Miss Saunders implies. Mallory's choice of Irvine for the final assault is a part of this, I'm sure. His words on the subject are evasive, though you must love someone deeply to take him with you to the top of Everest when his climbing experience is at the level of yours on your first trip to the Alps. The slope of love and death was already slippery for Mallory--Rupert Brooke's "forever England" and his ugly end in the Dardenelles; Wilfred Owen's homoerotic poems and his condemnation of a war that killed him a week before Armistice; Frances Darwin, the poet, and Gwen Darwin, the artist, and the survival of the fittest.

I sing it for him, the cut from Dylan's Blood on the Tracks. *It's a harsh, bitter tune about a relationship gone bad and the price of fame. On the surface his relationship with Ruth has never been in doubt. When they are engaged, he writes to his mother, "She's pure and loyal and courageous--all things precious to me." Just before their marriage on July 29, 1914, he tells Ruth, "I was deceiving myself to think that I could live without you" War breaks out a few days later, and on their honeymoon on the coast of Sussex they are held as German spies. Ten years later, in his last letter to her from Camp I, he tells her how much he loves her and says, "The candle is flickering, so I must end." But apparently things were not that simple between them.*

A spasm of what--disgust? shock? recognition?--crosses his face when my rasping voice cries out, I kissed goodbye the howling beast on the borderline that separated you from me. *The sharp arête between life and death, the dark heart of the Grail vision in which Galahad's terrible sense of his obsession cannot be glimpsed by the "beloved." Is there a beloved for the knight who can compare with Chomolungma, her unscalable manifestation in this world?*

"Why is he so angry, the man in the song?"

"Because he's been put on a pedestal, and he can't keep his balance anymore."

He blinks, and I lay my alpenstock over the crevasse between us. "Isn't it all a metaphor for Everest?"

"Whatever do you mean?"

"Idiot wind/blowin' through the buttons of our coats/blowin' through the letters that we wrote. *You write and write, and a white space is briefly marked with footprints of a kind. Your words are read weeks later by someone who doesn't know if you are still alive. The wind that rips at you now freezes her fingers in Cambridge later. She's meant to think,* It was gravity that pulled us in/ and destiny that drove us apart *when actually it's going to be the reverse."*

"I can't fathom any man speaking to a woman like that."

"Listen, listen to where you are in the words: What's good is bad/what's bad is good/when you reach the top/you find out/ you're on the bottom. *Come on, Galahad, you keep trying to move perfectly in such an imperfect world. Let's talk about some of the* images and distorted facts."

His appropriation when it comes is a complete surprise. I am looking over his shoulder. "Dear Ruth," he writes, I can't help it if I'm lucky.

Mobberley, Cheshire lies in the flight path of a proposed third runway for Manchester Airport. There are protest signs in the village. In the local pub, as if in anticipation of the inevitable, the woman tells me, "We don't do tea, dear, but I can make you some instant coffee." The church of St. Wilfrid and St. Mary is on the outskirts of the village, and seems to be closed. I cross the road to a shop and ask if there's anyone who can let me in. The clerks look at one another in secular dismay. "The church? You want to get into the church? Naw, sorry, love. Can't help." I am standing on tiptoe peeking through stained glass when an impeccably dressed woman comes out the front door and and says in a peremptory voice, "Can I help you?"

"Yes. I've come all the way from Canada to see the memorial in the church to George Mallory." Distance must lend importance, though I'm already shuddering at the borderlines that separate her from me. She is, it turns out, the rector's wife, a symbolic descendant of Mallory's mother, Annie Jebb, whose half-brother Jack had plans to search for Montezuma's treasure with Rider Haggard. In my leather jacket, with my three-week fringe of beard and long hair, I must seem an applicant for that expedition.

"Mallory," she says. "Yes, the air-marshall who died in the plane crash. There is a window."

"No, that was George's brother. George is the one who climbed Everest. *On* Everest."

"Well, come in. We'll have a look."

She is very proud of the recent reconstruction that has left much of the 14th-century nave intact. The carved wood curves above the altar like a distant plume of smoke. It is very cold. Our breaths congeal beneath the fiery sept of faith.

"Here it is," I say. The last window on the east side has three knights-errant: King Arthur, St. George, and, of course, Sir Galahad.

And these words: *All his life he sought after whatsoever things are Pure and High and Eternal. At last in the flower of his manhood, he was lost to human sight between Earth and Heaven on the topmost peak of Everest.* I scrawl them on the back of a brochure that reads "Llanberis Lodge, Snowdonia." Thanking her, I drive off towards Wales, in search of Pen-y-Pass and Mount Snowdon.

A few miles down the road I realize I have forgotten my glasses, which I took off in order to read the stained-glass inscription. She has returned to the all-new rectory, without trace of the old building where Mallory was born. She is alone, the rector out in the parish. Flustered by my reappearance when I had already receded comfortably into a tea-time story, the hirsute Canadian in pursuit of *that* Mallory, she strides out and shuts the door.

"My God, she announces, "I've left the keys inside!" British fortitude takes over immediately. "Come along, the sexton is there."

Sexton? Have I heard her correctly? Apparently so, for we find an old man tending some graves amidst the stones that lie scattered like so much moraine at time's feet. She opens the church door and waits. On a ledge below the window are my glasses. I retrieve them and remember how Mallory left things behind, signs that may have convinced others a flower grew between earth and heaven.

TWO

The aged man sits in the garden of the Llanberis Lodge at the very foot of Snowdon, watching the train wind up the back of the mountain like a red snake. He clears his throat, hawks up some flem, and spits. "Damn the tourists," he proclaims fiercely, as if his words will rise in the air to explode above the tracks, part of the battle he has declared and intends to win. It is April. Someone has brought him a wool blanket for protection against the strong spring breeze, but he has thrown it off at his feet. He sits in his wooden-wheeled chair like an ancient figure of state, staring down the questions I have brought. His name is Davies. He is 104 years old.

"Mallory," he says. "At first I didn't care much for him."

I have come here because he is the last of those who actually climbed with Mallory, at Pen-y-Pass before the War. A group of Cambridge youths had invaded the area in 1907, cavorting and screeching in streams and pools in the early mornings before setting off for their "exercise." At seventeen, already a veteran of Snowdon, Davies first saw Mallory with the others on the Terminal Arête of Lliwedd, a great buttress of the mountain.

"He was good at it, I'll say that, but there were times he didn't know when to stop."

He watched them scramble up the lower slopes, paying no attention to the rocks they were dislodging until one of near boulder-size rolled down to the edge of the dirt track where some locals were talking. He didn't separate Mallory out at that point, but a few days later there was cause to.

16

"He climbed the Slab on Lliwedd. Not easy. An exposed face with few holds. It was no problem for him. I knew he was a climber."

He stops, taking in deep breaths and gripping the edge of his wheels as if preparing for the next step up.

"But do you know why he went?"

I shake my head. Until now it has only been apocryphal.

"For a goddamn pipe! He'd left it on a ledge called the Bowling Green. Even though it was getting dark!" There is some admiration beneath the scorn.

"I've kissed some tricky faces in my time, but never for something that small." He laughs. "And some pretty ones too!"

"You did climb with him, though."

"Yes. Not then. It was a year or two later. We met over a meal at Gorphwysfa, the Rawson Owen hotel. Someone had told him I was the one to lead him up the Great Chimney. There were few of us knew the route back then. Certainly no Englishman!

We started out on a clear morning. He had his pipe and a small sack of food. I carried the rope. The rocks were dry most of the way, but it was a bit difficult on the ledge before the entrance. There's some seepage there, and the wall at head level pushes out, so you are leaning away while feeling for holds. It was balance climbing that demanded your attention every moment. We were tied together by then, of course, and I was leading, just a few feet ahead. Suddenly the rope came taut and I was almost jerked from my stance. I looked back, and there he was, standing with both hands free, lighting up! No warning, mind you. Just a thought for himself.

'What in God's name do you think you're doing?' I didn't yell, which is what I wanted to do, because *I* didn't want to start *him*. He looks at me very coolly. 'Just coming, dear fellow,' is what he said, as if he had stopped for a moment in the high street.

Now there are those who will tell you he was never reckless and that he must have had great respect for my abilities when he fired that pipe, but I say that's nonsense! He overreached himself then, and he nearly took us both down. That's what happened on Everest."

17

"What do you mean?"

"He told me." As if no great secret has been revealed. As if he were casually pulling Icarus from the sea.

Davies has been patient. No one has interviewed him before. He has been waiting for me for almost half a century, storing up the memories, transforming them into a tale needing only readers to be true.

"Odell found him at Camp VI. His face was broken from a fall. The ice had dug grooves in it like so many crevasses. He must have been in terrible pain. But he was quiet. That was what bothered Odell the most. He couldn't get him to say a word. Not about what had happened, not about Irvine. Mallory had the axe in his hands, the one they found in '33. He wouldn't let go, no matter how much Odell pried at his fingers. The face was a mess, but there was no bleeding, not at that height, so Odell brewed some tea and made him drink it. They sat there in silence in that little tent at 26,700 feet, the world's most revered climber and the man who should have tried for the summit with him. Later, Odell would remember that it seemed perfectly natural for awhile, as if they were gathering strength for an assault. As they were, though not on that peak that lay above them, so benign in the morning light that it seemed but a stroll's distance away.

'We have to go down, George.'

Mallory's gloves slowly uncurl from the handle. The axe drops on his knees and slides to the groundsheet. 'I killed him.'

Odell hears the words like the sound of a bullet that has grazed his skull. The only thing he knows is that he is still alive. He must have said, 'What?' or 'What happened to Irvine?' Such words would have made sense. He recalled reaching across to Mallory to touch his arm. That's when he became violent. He kicked out savagely at Odell, at the same time bringing down one of the tent supports. Odell felt he was drowning in a canvas sea, his heavy clothes dragging at him as he tried to surface, Mallory's screams the pressure on his eardrums. It was all he could do to extricate himself from that mess. And just as suddenly it was over. No more

18

movement, no more noise. Odell knew he needed help. He placed a sleeping bag over Mallory, who was breathing quietly, in the still-upright half of the tent, and descended to Camp IV where Hazard was waiting

Imagine this climb down for Odell. The day before he thought he had glimpsed them both at what he took to be the Second Step. Mallory 'was not daunted by the impossible,' someone had said, and he had instilled that sense of what could be done in everyone else, so Odell had gone to VI fully expecting to find them, tired certainly and in need of oxygen, but conquerors at last. Instead there was this horror of enigma and violence, and most of all, of those appalling words that he struggled to repress, so vivid were the possibilities they evoked, the distress they promised to share.

He shook Hazard awake. 'I've found Mallory.' *He's gone mad,* he almost said, but bit his tongue. 'He's badly hurt. No sign of Irvine.'

They climbed back up, but he was gone, the trail leading towards the First Step. The sun wasn't on them, and it was very cold as they strained upwards towards the Northeast Ridge. There was always the danger of frostbite, and the moment the sun did appear, they took off their outer gloves and held up their hands in supplication, rubbing them vigorously together. They found him crouched about sixty feet below the crest of the ridge and some two hundred yards east of the Step. The axe was at his feet, but in their anxiety for him they ignored it, and so unintentionally contributed to the mystery that would save them all.

But they couldn't ignore the crimson stain on the rock he now held. 'George,' Odell said quietly, 'what happened?' And he stood up. 'I am ready now,' he replied. He would say nothing else for twenty-two years.

They looked around for Irvine, of course, but there was nothing. Nothing but the summit plume above them, and the certain knowledge they would die if they stayed any longer.

So they got him down to Norton, their snowblind leader who, with Somervell, was at Camp III. It took many hours, including a stopover at IV. Mallory moved with his usual grace over difficult slopes. Since few, if any, words were possible under such conditions, it was only his riven face that told a tale.

Norton was a good man. They were all *good* men, you know, but he had more mettle inside than most. You don't go into the Great Couloir alone because you mean well. If he was badly shaken by what Odell tried to tell him in the first few minutes, it wasn't for the reasons you'd think. They bundled Mallory up in sleeping bags, and gave him some soup, which he ate without protest. When he didn't respond to Norton's repeated addresses to him, they all sat down together around the stove outside, Norton wearing a kind of blindfold to protect his injured eyes.

'It wasn't a conspiracy, at least not from the start,' Odell told me at Pen-y-Gwryd. This was two years later. There was a gale blowing, and no one else was at the hotel, except the woman who cooked and the boy who took care of the rooms. We were at a table beneath the ceiling that Mallory, Geoffrey Young, and Graham Irving had signed in better days. In a farmhouse a few miles beyond the Pass, Mallory was sitting by the fire, his facial wounds healed into disfiguring scars that made him virtually unrecognizable, his silence unbroken.

'We sat in stunned disarray,' Odell said. 'Here was the finest climber we had ever known, a man of unassailable character, his wife and children--the whole country!-- waiting at home, changed utterly in appearance and mind, bereft of the glory he had sought, conjuring the spectre of death on Everest in the most unimaginable terms.' Minutes passed, the tent snapping in the wind, the slurp of tea through lips that sought the warmth of assuredness, existence on the tongue. Finally Norton spoke.

'Let's go through this again. You thought you saw them both at the Second Step, and then you found Mallory alone. What went on up there? What did he say, exactly?'

Odell didn't respond right away. When the others looked at him, he was weeping, the tears melting the snow on his boot tops. 'He was sitting in the tent at VI. His face was frightful. I told him we had to go down. He said...' A pause. Then three words that rang in that immense space with the surprising delicacy of bells in the monastery at Rongbuk. *'I killed him.'*

'But surely he didn't mean...' Somervell's first attempt.

'Anything else?' Norton cutting him off.

'Yes, after we found him again near the First Step, he stood up and said, "I am ready now."' *'I am ready now,'* Odell repeated softly, with the slightest trace of interrogation, as if bewildered by the incantatory impact of the words.

Hazard spoke. 'We have to get him down to a hospital. That face needs attention.'

'Yes,' said Norton. 'Then what?'

'I don't understand,' Hazard replied. 'We take him home. His mind will clear.'

'And if it doesn't?'

'It was much worse in the War. Plenty of men went home and wouldn't say a word, and plenty of them were marked up badly, too.'

'Mallory was there. Remember? Afterwards, he was still the man we knew. We need to consider this.'

Somervell stood up. 'What is it you're talking about, Norton? Be plain.'

The others could feel the impact of Norton's gaze through the cloth cover, as if he were staring at the bright snow on the moraine rocks without flinching. "What if it's true?" he said. "What if he killed Irvine?'

'Good God, man!' Somervell recoiled as if struck.

'Teddy, Teddy. How can you ask that?' Hazard cried.

Odell said nothing. Nothing until Norton addressed him directly. 'Noel?'

They looked at Odell. It was testimony they wanted. 'He was holding Irvine's axe when he told me. There was blood on the rock where we found him later.'

'And the axe? Where's the axe?' Norton was fierce now.

'Up there. By the First Step.'

Clouds had settled over the glacier above them. They knew that no one, even if there *were* oxygen available, could go back over the seven thousand feet of ice and snow-covered slabs between now and then.

'We can't take him home in the open,' Norton said. 'We can't have him speaking of killing to reporters and the Committee. There are Ruth and the children, as well.'"

Davies snorts derisively. "What he really meant was the Empire. The bloody British Empire. The others knew it, too. Couldn't have this paragon who was born to be knighted--and would've been too if he'd triumphed--airing some dirty mountain linen in public. All those old Royal Geographical farts, and the bloody King, too, never liked to think of the weeks on the mountain in the same underclothes, the greasy hair, and foul bodies and breath that you could smell in a crowded tent! It was all meant to be white like the snow. Fresh powder every morning and no trace of piss!"

"You helped them, though."

He looks at me tenderly, as if I were a child trying to climb into his lap, but too small to do so unassisted.

"In the end, I was all they had. Besides, when I finally saw him I thought he might have to talk eventually. He was working it out inside. It was like watching a man who is stalled on a difficult pitch. You can't reach him. You daren't speak and break his concentration. But you know if he is good, he will come through. I was prepared to wait."

I make some tea on the gas stove in his kitchen. It is such a simple task. The flame flares up and dies with ease.

"Norton deserves a lot of the credit, if that's what you want to call it. He was trying to have a few climbers live out what those who ran the show had done for centuries. Do you think Nelson really died the way the dispatches said? When Tennyson glorified that crazy charge in the Crimea he was Poet Laureate, wasn't he? Government lackey more like it!"

I recall *The Death of Wolfe* by Benjamin West, court painter. The sweet expiration while a seemingly pensive Indian, the Canadian coolie who was never there, looks on, not thinking of the price his people will pay for *this* expedition. For West, not thinking at all.

They argued through the afternoon, Davies told me. At least Somervell and Hazard did in desultory fashion, wandering over the face of a peak so big they never saw its top. It was Teddy Norton-- and Odell, with his unspeaking acquiescence--who organized everything. They had already dismissed the porters, who had started back to India the day before. Norton and Somervell would go down to base camp and tell the others there was no trace of the summit pair. And this is where they came up with their magnificent story, the myth of Mallory and Irvine that would deflect attention away from any alternative, from a deeper mystery, and a shadowy figure on the boat from Bombay to Liverpool.

"You shouldn't be surprised by the task they set for themselves," he says. "It's not how they did it that matters. It's why."

THREE

"You saw them. Going strong for the top. Write it down." It is an order from a Lieutenant-Colonel in the Royal Horse Artillery, given with calm authority and the expectation of obedience, and Odell knows this. In his tent that night he brings the stark necessity into focus, and composes that remarkable passage, a paean to Galahad and his noble companion that interns them forever in stained-glass reverence:

Between Camps V and VI I had stopped to search for fossil rocks, and happened to look up as the final stretch of ridge leading to the summit was suddenly unveiled in sunlight. There, on what could only have been the Second Step, given my angle of vision, I saw two small dots, one at the top of the step and one moving slowly towards its base. Then the clouds closed in, and it was the last I saw of Mallory and Irvine.

So he put them at the Second Step, at 28,230 feet, beyond debate, he thought, for no man had seen it except at a distance. Norton had looked up at it from the Great Couloir on June 3. No one else would get closer for thirty-six years, and then the two Chinese and the Tibetan, who would claim the first ascent by the Northeast Ridge, foolishly or conveniently arrived on the summit in the dark, so there were no photographs.

In 1993 an Irish climber engaged the Second Step and used the ladder left hanging by a second Chinese expedition. It took everything Seamus Byrne had to climb the rock wall, including a radio connection to base camp and two litres of oxygen a minute in a container that weighed 3.2 kilos, as compared with the 14 kilos that the 1924 climbers carried on their backs. Byrne is adamant that Mallory and Irvine could not have climbed *this* step, given its difficulty, their relatively primitive gear, and the absence of the ladder. Others before him, pronouncing through telescopes, insisted that Odell must have meant the *First* Step, that no mortal could have ascended the Second Step without his companion in support directly below him. But the journal entry did buy a lot of time, and it did preoccupy divided groups of Everest acolytes who wanted either to canonize Mallory or put a stake of ice through his heart.

Davies doesn't seem to tire, as if he is on oxygen and the altitude is of no account.

"Odell showed it to Norton the next morning," he tells me.

"'Good. It is what George would have liked. It shows him higher than us all.'

Norton and Somervell descended with the bad news for the base camp crew. They were shocked, of course, but asked few questions. Norton told them of Odell's sighting, providing little detail. He told them to head back to Sikkim and from there to Darjeeling. He, Somervell, Hazard, and Odell would build a cairn memorial in the Rongbuk Valley. It would commemorate Mallory and Irvine, as well as those porters who had died on the 1921 and 1922 expeditions. He also told them he'd send a cable to the Royal Geographical Society. Which he did, by runner. Norton was a cool one. Stuck to the pre-arranged code so as not to arouse any suspicion.. Do you know what it said? *Mallory Irvine Nove Remainder Alcedo, Norton Rongbuk*. The world knew on June 20.

God knows what that one-month trip through Tibet and India must have involved. Odell said it was hell because nothing happened, though they were all keyed for an explosion. It was like the War when everything went quiet and you waited for the sound of the shell that had your name on it. They were also carrying the knowledge of what they were doing. It wasn't a load you could shrug off at night. In fact, it got heavier then, especially as they got closer to civilization. What kinds of questions would be asked? Could they keep their stories in tune? They'd memorized Odell's piece, of course. And they could each swear with absolute conviction and authority as to the last time they'd seen Mallory and Irvine before the pair left on their summit drive. It was Odell who'd brought them the news. After that they couldn't do anything else but pack up and get out. The mountain had won.

Meanwhile, Norton had sent dispatches to the expedition sponsors in London, documenting everything that had taken place from their time of arrival at base camp, through the unsuccessful assault by himself and Somervell, and the story of the final attempt. It was an avalanche of paper, and what got buried wasn't always found. But it had the result he wanted. Something Hinks of the RGS wrote to Mrs. Bruce, the wife of the Everest Committee chairman, lets you know that. I never forgot it because it showed how the crossover in Norton's mind between what happened and what he wanted to have happened affected all the others: Hinks said that Odell's witnessing of the pair 'elevates the matter altogether, and turns us from calamity to brilliant attainment.'

They got Mallory on the boat at Bombay. Things were lax in those days. Norton and Somervell did the press conference, while Odell and Hazard stayed back with him at the hotel. It took a bribe at night to get him on board, but once that was done, it was smooth sailing. There was one more person Norton needed, though, and he telegraphed him to meet the ship at Gibraltar. Geoffrey Young.

Mohammed coming to the mountain. That's what it was. Too much of the poet and lordly air about him for me, but he was a pioneer, I'll give him that. New routes in the Alps before the turn of the century, and hard rock-climbing feats at home that turned all our heads. He came down to Llanberis and the Pass when I was a boy and took Lliwedd like a virgin bride. He respected the hills, loved them, I'd say, but he always let them know who was in charge. I think he wrote a lot of rubbish about Mallory before and after Everest, but if you like books on climbing then *Snowdon Biography* is what you're after. I'm in it somewhere. We got stuck on a ledge once on Craig yr Cwm Dhu."

I try to imagine them together there, the second son of a baronet who met Mallory at the Charles Lamb dinner at Cambridge, and the Welsh ferrier's son who hits away at pretence as his father must have gone at the anvil. Young was supposed to have had the common touch, and tremendous respect for physical expression, so he must have felt comfortable with his countrified and vigorous Welsh companion. But I suspect, for all his Trinity College intellect and training, he didn't read the book of Davies as carefully as he did his beloved Elizabethan sonnets.

In late June of 1924, Young must have been dizzy from not only the loss but also the *failure* of Mallory. He had been convinced his protégé would succeed. In his July obituary he would give no hint of disappointment:

George Mallory, or 'Sir Galahad' as his fellow climbers dubbed him, pursued his grail selflessly and in a manner that inspired all who knew him and the world besides. Everest itself--at once dreadful and resplendent-- shall be his everlasting memorial, as will the Bard's immortal words: 'He was a man, take him for all in all. I shall not look upon his like again.'

To Ruth he said, "I cannot put into mere words what his shining example meant to me. His was a victory over all adversity, and the essence of his ascent will endure forever." It was over the top stuff. He was completely committed to the myth, and couldn't retreat. Which is why I can't dismiss what Davies tells me. Gradually, his words become my words.

Young was only too happy to meet Norton at Gibraltar. He'd read the dispatches, but like that shell at Monte San Gabriele they'd burst in fragments and damaged him severely, only this time it was not his leg that had been amputated. He needed desperately to talk to, to touch, someone who been *there*. Most of all, he wanted to see Odell. That journal entry of the last sighting haunted him. If there had been no war, and he'd been ten years younger he would have been on Everest from the beginning. And no question about the final pairing.

Norton was waiting for him in his cabin, a tall, shadowy figure who would retire one day with the rank of Lieutenant-General. Young had to stand on the toes of his right leg to embrace him.

"Teddy..."

"Sit down, Geoffrey." Young obeyed. It was a voice from above. But whatever message he was expecting to glissade into his heart it was not the one he heard now.

"He's alive."

Yes, thought Young. He *is!* In all of us.

Norton knew by his smile that Young had not understood. He had to shock the man, to cut through the storied clouds of glory, to begin the *real* story. "He says he killed Irvine."

Young blinked. Lying in that Italian mud, concussed, the pain circling him like a buzzard, he'd had an out-of-body experience. He saw himself face down by that little stream-bank under the continuing hail of fire, and knew if he stayed there he would die. His own voice called out to him, gently but firmly, urging him to crawl, to move by inches and moments, to a place where everything would become whole again. Whether he actually changed his position, he never found out, but *inside* he dragged himself toward that promised land, and when he awoke in the hospital tent he discovered he had made a bargain to enter it by degrees for the rest of the life he had won. Norton's words were a burning cross to be clasped on the road to Zion. "Where is he?" he said.

"Here, on the ship. But he's not himself. He hasn't spoken, not a word, since Odell brought him down from above VI. And, there's something else, Geoffrey." Norton sensed that *this* change in Galahad might be the worst. "He's terribly disfigured. The ice savaged his face."

"I'll go to him, Teddy." There would be no questions about Odell's sighting or the dispatches to London. Young recognized

28

their mythic proportions, how vital they were in measurement against the incarnate.

They walked down the passage in silence. It was a labyrinth of deception they were entering, roped together with no trailing threads to trip them up, moving towards a creature they must assail with love.

He was standing by the tiny, open porthole gazing at the sea, its sheen like verglass in the Mediterranean sun. "George," Young said softly, and there was no reponse, except for an almost imperceptible shudder caused, perhaps, by the ripple of a breeze that touched their faces as they stood behind him. Young took him by the shoulder and turned him round. The scars were cold to his touch. He held his breath as he traced with his fingers the fissures they now hid. He wept openly as he held the precious grail in his hands for the first and only time, the quest, like Galahad himself, tarnished beyond redress. But Young was a climber as well as a dreamer. "What did he say to Odell?"

"That he killed Irvine. That was in the tent at VI. He was holding Irvine's axe. He became violent when Odell suggested they descend. So he left him there and went down to Hazard for help. They found him up near the First Step with a bloody rock in his hands. There was no sign of Irvine. He said, 'I am ready now.'"

"He couldn't have killed him."

"But he thinks he did. I think if he is pressed, he will say it again."

Young sat down. Mallory had turned back to the window. "You were right to do it, Teddy."

There was no need for them to justify anything to themselves. It was Mallory they were saving, for a world that needed to be saved in this way.

They talked for a long time, making no attempt to lower their voices in deference to the man-child at the porthole. There were five of them who knew now. Odell would be directly involved, if only by virtue of his unveiled vision. No, that was unfair. He had suffered on that mountain with the first discovery, as they had not done. Norton thought Somervell and Hazard, having come this far, would just want to go home and forget, though the former had kept a journal which the RGS would want to see, and would have to fill in the last pages accurately (the term was no longer an ironic one to them). No one else would be involved. Their alliance was necessarily small and based on matter as firm and pointed as the rock of empire that stood not a hundred yards from their cabin door. All five of them were climbers. Four of them had been higher on earth than any *living* man; the fifth, according to most, was the most significant influence on British mountaineering of his remarkable generation. There was no room for those who had not essayed such heights, and that could only mean, of course, any living *man*.

Young felt anguish for Ruth Mallory, for the loss of her husband, and the father of her children. She had done some climbing in Wales, but she had not wanted Mallory to go on this last expedition, and had written Young just days ago: "Oh Geoffrey, it wasn't inevitable. What could we have done to prevent it?" By this, he felt, she was not alluding to the chance of slip or bad weather, but of Mallory's having gone back to Everest for the third time. And then she had said the words that confirmed in his mind now it was a far better thing for her to keep the myth intact: "But he was ready to go on. His soul was ready, and the manner of his leaving us was radiant and true. Out of it all we may find a blessed repose." Quietly, resolutely, the door of the brotherhood was closed. Or so they thought.

They would take him back to North Wales, and find someone to look after him, an older woman who could care less that Snowdon was at her doorstep. They never thought of him 'waking up,' except in the darkest sense, into nightmare (theirs and his). In those days, madness of such magnitude was not a thing to be remedied, but a fatal, lingering illness that doctors studied and patients endured. The George Mallory they had known *was* dead. His memory must be revered, and part of that memory was frozen forever in this mute, diminished figure before them. If his tongue ever loosened and he began to babble one of them should be summoned immediately. Only then would they decide how to meet such a threat. The only alternative--Davies particularly loved this part--was to kill *Mallory*! It must have crossed both their minds, but was immediately covered by an avalanche of unspeakable guilt and shame. So they picked up a grail of another kind, a cup of trembling, from which they drank deep and long. Twenty-two years while Galahad lived, and another decade or two after that for four of the five brothers. Odell became a professor and outlasted them all. He was still answering questions over sixty years later when his clouds closed in. "That," Davies says, "left me."

"I must admit it took the wind out of my sails," he says. "Third time lucky, you know. I suppose I expected, after the reconnaissance in '21 and Finch and Bruce getting above 27,000 feet the next year, that they'd make it. And by "they," all of us back here meant Mallory. It was easy for us to flit around on Snowdon--not that you can't die up there (he gestures almost tenderly to the peak that is really no more than a large hill by Alpine or Himalayan standards), but anything you can climb in a day doesn't kill *you*. And besides, you can't disappear, at least not for long. They'll find you in the scree, like as not."

I've got no time for amateurs, he was telling me. I could see my body in his mind's eye, falling from the steep, white page into the detritus of footnotes below.

"And Mallory?" I ask. "Was he an amateur too?" If he notices the adverb, he doesn't let on.

"In some ways, yes. Amateurs are self-centered, and he was that. But he had the gift. He was pure joy to watch when he moved. Didn't amount to much when he stood still; at least I didn't think so, not for a long time."

There's a scene in *Butch Cassidy and the Sundance Kid* that I tell him about. Butch and the Kid are trying to get a job as mine payroll guards in Bolivia. The mine owner asks the Kid if he can handle a gun (like asking Mallory if he can use an ice-axe). "Yeah," says the Kid. "Can you hit that?" the owner asks, pointing to a tin can or something similar lying on the ground about fifty feet away. "Okay," the Kid tells him. He draws his colt and fires several shots; all of them are wide of the mark. As the owner is walking away in disgust, the Kid says, "Can I move?" "Can you move?" the owner replies. "Why of course you can move. What kind of a dumb question is that?" So the Kid dives to his right, drawing his gun, rolling over in the dirt, and firing at the same time. The can is perforated. Butch and the Kid get the job.

Davies laughs so hard I think he will topple from his chair. Beads of sweat pop out on his forehead, and he pulls an old, red handkerchief from his pocket. "Exactly," he says, coughing into his hand. "And that's why Mallory kept getting the job. No one else went to Everest three times. All he had to do when the RGS bigwhigs looked his way was *move*."

Norton and Young brought him to Pen-y-Pass that summer. Young had gone back by train after the meeting on the boat, and found an old farm in the hills. It wasn't a local woman they got for him, but a German widow who'd come here after the War. Mrs. Bergschund was from Lubeck, right up on the Baltic Sea flats near Denmark. Hills, especially large ones, were an aberration to her. I'm sure she'd never heard of Everest. (Davies gets a malicious little smile on his face at this point. "When asked why," he says, she was reported to have replied, "Because it wasn't there"). She was told that Mallory, whom they called Jones, a good, unsuspicious Welsh name, had been afflicted by the War and needed only peace and isolation. After all, Mallory had written to a Cambridge friend on the eve of his departure for India, "This time it will be a war against the mountain. I may not survive." He hadn't spoken since the onset of his trauma, so it would be of great interest to Mr. Norton and Mr. Young, and to a certain Mr. Odell, if he did. They left telephone numbers and strict instructions to call at any time of day or night.

It got tricky occasionally, what with Norton off on army assignment in India before the second War and then as Governor of Hong Kong before it fell to the Japanese. Odell, of course, was still climbing. He went back to Everest in '38, and two years before that climbed Nanda Devi with Henry Tilman, a record peak for fourteen years until the French took Annapurna. Young's leg kept him fairly close to home throughout, though he liked to go off to the Alps every once in awhile. They soon realized that they needed someone in on the secret who could handle Mr. Jones quickly and effectively if the need arose, and who could be trusted to be discreet. But who was there locally who fit the bill? In other words, who was a novitiate for the brotherhood with all its birthright requirements and attendant regulations? 'Not me, that was for damn sure!'" Davies yells it out, and I hear the echoes resound among the long-abandoned ruins beyond the Pass.

"I never paid any attention to it: Mrs. Bergschund, the farm occupied after years of disuse. There's never been much gossip hereabouts. People have better things to do. Norton and Young knew that. After the War"--he catches me looking at him--"Yes, I was there too. We all were. Gunboats alongside the merchant ships, ferrying supplies across the Channel. After the War, I took up guiding fulltime. Lots of bloody amateurs then, weekenders, toffs down from London, but it was better than the mines or driving a lorry in Bangor. Kept me busy, what with devising new rescue routes, and learning to talk scared boys and girls into putting one foot or hand in front of the other. I was an amateur of sorts myself, in psychology, that is. They opened up once they got above sea level. Life stories that either had me in stitches or left me wondering what the world was coming to. And we got the answer soon enough, didn't we? They all wanted to talk about their nasty parents or love or what they were going to do one day, never a word about here and now, the way the rocks glistened in the sun after a cloudburst, the smell of heather, the heft of a rope in your hand as you coiled it for the climb. Like Mallory, in a way. Always going on in his heyday about what he felt about the mountain, never how he climbed it."

He's right; it's just that Mallory felt that climbers who didn't try to come to terms with *why* they put their lives in danger were "desperate men, very much like outlaws who would pay the price one day." I don't say this, however. I want him to keep talking.

"Young came to me in the winter of '26. It was cold. I wasn't doing much but sitting by the fire, mending equipment, and occasionally taking someone with a bit of knowhow out on the verglass. I hadn't seen him for quite awhile, certainly not since the Everest climbs began. The whole mob of them came down in 1919. That's when Young wrote this." He hands me a tattered piece of yellowed paper: *Broken before my time/My dreams yet one/I turn toward the hills./To past and future climbs/The summits call me still.* "A lot of romantic nonsense, I thought then. But now I'm a hundred and more, I don't know." He looks at me with his bright, blue eyes, and for a moment his guard is down.

"He knocked on my door and entered at my bidding. He hadn't changed. The same strong features, the same moustache over a chiseled mouth and chin. He was fifty years old.

'Davies.'

That was always his address, just as my response was always 'Mr. Young.' For him it was class; for me it was upbringing. I didn't feel inferior, and if he felt any better than me, it was nothing personal.

'I've something to tell you,' he said. 'Something that will no doubt shock you. But I have come to you for help because you are a man we can trust.'

I didn't know who the *we* were, but I soon found out I'd heard of them all. Though I never met Somervell and Hazard. When he told me that Mallory was alive and living not five miles from where we sat, I almost lost my nerve. By that I mean I almost blubbered out something thoughtless. But he was measuring me carefully as he spoke, and I was determined he'd pay for every inch.

I listened to the story of Odell's encounters, the plans made at Camp III and subsequent bulletins to the world--which only heightened my already strong respect for Norton, based on his climbs. Then I heard about the meeting at Gibraltar. Young didn't attempt to explain why so much was being done for one man, though he did emphasize the hopes and aspirations that Mallory had been carrying on his shoulders. I think he knew that I bloody well understood the brotherhood, just as we both understood that I could never be a *bona fide* member, nor would want to be. But it was for them a kind of reaching out to the common climber, if you like, and this was a new concept. It was one thing to trust someone with your life, but quite another to hand him your reputation.

I'll admit it was his vulnerability that first attracted me to his proposal, his *and* Mallory's. I've already told you, it's the physical details of a climb that matter to me. Here were five of the best mountaineers alive, in *courte-échelle* on a ledge, with Mallory at the top of the pyramid. There was no way up or down. They wanted to be assured of staying there, to avoid any "calamity" of their own making, and I was the vital support man whom they couldn't predict or deny.

Young took me over to the farm. It lay at the end of a winding track beneath Graig Dhu and looked out on Llyn Idwal. Straight up the earth went from the back of the outbuildings, and in front the waters blue as sky. I thought I knew what to expect. I'd pulled men I'd known from the Channel, burned by oil and coughing up their lungs, salt in the great, raw wound of their bodies. Not a trace of what once and laughed and danced with me in the smokestack lee. But this was different. It was George Mallory alright. Just from the way he rose from his chair and walked to the window you could tell that. In his very adaption to the space around him, the proportions of his life confined by the hearth, the whitewashed stone walls, and the small cache of basic items provided for his comfort, he retained that harmony with his immediate environment that had always been his saving grace as far as I was concerned. Even the fissures on his face didn't break the accord. Oh, I know all about Strachey's ravings and young Mallory's turning of Virginia Stephen's head, but looks don't help you on a spillikin's sharp edge. What I wasn't prepared for was the utter absence of that Mallory who had been so maddening to me, the one who thought too much and talked too much about himself in the mountains, whose ego was a pitch so much steeper than those he climbed. He was purely *physical* now. The alchemist just an element himself. That's what I thought on the first day and for a long time after.

'George, you remember Davies. He'll be looking in on you now and then.'

He turned and swept me with those eyes that seemed to take in everything and nothing at once. They saw me alright, but against a backdrop of some implacable contours I could not fathom. It was then I wondered if he had killed Irvine. Remember, I disapproved of a lot about Mallory, and beneath that civilized shell we grow around ourselves, there is in each of us a deadly kernel of self-assertion. In him that kernel was overripe. If Irvine thwarted him when they were within reach of the summit, if Mallory thought the boy could have made it but *would* not, there may have been an explosion sparked by the honourable need to descend together and the rigid desire to succeed. I was judgemental about that, but I was not prepared to condemn him without trial. For any verdict to be returned, *he* had to testify. And that wasn't going to happen easily. Young and Norton had seen to it. This farmhouse cell was where he was meant to live out his days.

So our relationship began. If you had told me then that our journey together would take twenty-two years and would end in its way on Everest itself, I would have laughed and waved you aside. Young and Norton offered me a stipend for my services, but I declined. I would not be bound by any kind of contract, except the one that contained things unspoken, which would never have been admitted in that aborted trial.

At first I would go over twice a week, Wednesdays and Saturdays usually, for the afternoon. It gave Mrs. Bergschund some time away. She would have a few things in for tea, and I would sit by the fire and talk to him. Something had to be done to break the silence. I was uncomfortable when he didn't respond to my basic comments about the weather and Mrs. Bergschund's cooking. I couldn't ask him about his health, how he was *feeling*, could I? He looked well enough. I found out that he walked everyday down to the lake and along the shore. He never climbed nor gave any indication of wanting to do so. When that finally happened I wasn't expecting it at all. Anyway, like I said, I talked, and he did seem to listen.

And I read to him. Mrs. Bergschund said she put the local paper in front of him every other day, and Young sent *The Times* once a week. But he pushed them politely aside. I wondered what sustained him, his mind, I mean. After all, he was at Cambridge, he knew all those intellectuals, and he had been a master at Charterhouse. Cottie Sanders told me he couldn't be bested in an argument because of the moral soundness of his position and because he never lost his temper. He could be somewhat prudish, she said, about matters of right and wrong, but even if he was outdone in debating skills, his principles and the spirit behind them were never shaken. And Somervell said in his book that Mallory liked nothing better than a good exchange. So I was perplexed by the absence of any mental stimulation. It wasn't until much later that he began to write.

Young told me one of his favourite books was Bridges' *The Spirit of Man*. He especially liked the 'Epitaph to Gray's Elegy,' which I did read aloud. But some of those lines were too much for me--I stammered a little when I got to 'the paths of glory lead but to the grave,' but he didn't seem to notice. Once, on a visit, Young quoted that bit about the 'mute and glorious Milton,' though he said it with great sadness, as he did those final lines from *Prometheus Unbound*. Something like 'hoping until hope creates/from its own wreck/the thing it contemplates.' I thought the Milton comparison overdone, but the Shelley rang true enough.

I read him novels that Young recommended--*The Woman in White*, Galsworthy's *The Country House*, some George Eliot and Dickens. Virginia Woolf's *To the Lighthouse*. Young said Mallory was somewhere in Lily Briscoe's painting. Not in the boat with Mr. Ramsay and the kids because he never actually got to the lighthouse, you see. It was the aspiration she was after, Young insisted.

There were others books I never asked Young about. One got Mallory very agitated, but when I put it down he pushed it back toward me. He got up and paced as I read, and when it was done, he took the book and put in in the hearth. He didn't throw it, but placed it gently, as if it was a gift for the fire. It was a new book, published the year after he came to the Pass. *The Great Gatsby* it was called. American writer. Do you know it? I thought about his response, and it seemed to me it had to do with those lines from Gray's 'Epitaph.' Remember the ladder Gatsby thinks he can climb to the stars? Just like Everest for Mallory. And then it's *sic transit gloria mundi*, whatever the purity of your motives. He must have been grappling with that. You see the education I was given during those years.

I also read him Graves's *Goodbye to All That* when it caused such a fuss in 1929. Graves had been a student at Charterhouse, you know, and had climbed with Mallory on Snowdon. He said Mallory was his first real friend, and wrote to his wife after he disappeared that Mallory had confided in him that when he died he wanted to be on a mountain.. Mallory had been best man at Graves's wedding, so they must have been close. In the book, I don't think Graves mentions staying with Ruth Mallory after he was wounded in France, but he did.

When he went to France, Mallory was behind the trenches with an artillery position, but then he went into the front lines because communications had broken down between the guns and the spotters. Men were killed right beside him, just as with Graves, so I'm sure he knew what that part of the book was about. What I don't think he liked was Graves leaving England the way he did, becoming an expatriate down in Spain. But only Mallory could have climbed the the White Spider on the Eiger and taken *The White Goddess* in his pack. That's what Young said.

There was one I didn't read to him. Young advised against it when he brought it to me, though he didn't need to. I knew David Pye from his visits to the Pass and Pen-y-Gwryd just before the War. In the winter of 1914, we went up Snowdon in a storm, four of us roped together. Mallory in front, his wife behind, then David and me. We could hardly breathe in the wind and soon realized we couldn't go on. The snow slope on the lee side of the ridge was our way down, but Ruth Mallory wouldn't make the leap. And who could blame her? Unless you knew better you were jumping to your death. Mallory just took her hand firmly and jumped with her over the edge. David and I anticipated this and held the rope firm. What she must have thought at that moment! I think David writes about it in his biography, the one I kept to myself. *George Leigh Mallory* he called it. I remember something else he wrote, though I'm not sure it was in the book. Even if it wasn't, it was the kind of thing Pye said there. *For Mallory, controlled physical expression amidst the vagaries of the natural world represented spiritual accomplishment for oneself and any human witness.* Perhaps he wouldn't have minded that. But it was all the eulogies, his life wrapped in a winding sheet, that we didn't think he should hear.

When I didn't read, I talked. Mostly about myself. What else was there? I suppose over the years he heard my life story, though he got it in fragments. Chapters that didn't run together. Memories that went back on themselves. All the editing we do when we sum up. You know I was born in 1890. In Lampeter, Dyfed. That's in the hills, inland from Aberayron. It's an old market town on the River Teifi that floods every spring. There's also a college there, St. David's, which put me in good company with Mallory because after Oxford and Cambridge, it's the oldest in Britain. I never went there, of course.

My father was a ferrier, an ironsmith you'd call him. Shod the horses for the farmers about, mended their machinery, and even did up fancy gates for the wealthier ones. I helped out in the shop while I was still in school and in the holidays. The best of us usually didn't get much beyond six or eight years of lessons. My older brothers stopped before that, and my sister was married off at fifteen to a hodder in the next village. But my parents saw I liked to read. I'd bring books home from the school and then from the town library that was used to catering to the St. David's boys. Nothing special, mind you. Just adventure books and some history, though I did like *Silas Marner* and *Great Expectations* when I found them. Ask me sometime how I got hold of *The Way of All Flesh*. It was banned from the library, you know. But all good things come to an end. There was never any thought of my attending St. David's. It was another world altogether. So at fourteen I entered my father's trade. It was interesting enough, and I suppose I would have stayed there. But the next summer I went off on a bit of a ramble in the hills up north, and that was that.

I walked with my pack on my back up through Beddgelert and Capel Curig and on to Pen-y-Gwryd. It was wild country then. Not like this tourist haven. You could go for miles along the roads and not see a soul. I came to the top of the Pass in a storm of lightning and hail and found Gorphwysfa. I hadn't done any climbing, not beyond a quarry cliff or two, and those in the best of conditions. But when the sky cleared and I saw Snowdon, I knew what I wanted to do.

Rawson Owen was good to me. After I'd gone home and had it out with my father, whom I did hurt because now there'd be no one to take over the shop, I came back and worked at the hotel, cleaning up at first, but then helping to organize the climbs and walking excursions. Any spare time I had I was up that hill, learning to traverse, to shift backwards up chimneys, to rappel and belay. I was mostly on my own, which is good for the confidence if you can handle it, but it leaves you a bit impatient with others, especially when they think they know it all. I learned too from some of the old guides who thought Snowdon was the rock of ages in which they could put their faith, more than was ever found in the Church of Wales, I can tell you.

In two years I was able to go up and down with the best of them, though I was never a lad who ran on at the mouth about anything. I never bragged about what I could do. Rawson Owen would have had my head, and so, eventually, would Snowdon. That's when I first climbed with Young and Mallory, though there were plenty of veterans who came through for the practice on rock faces they would do on the Chamonix Aiguilles or even in the Dolomites. There were some foreigners like Blodig who'd done all the 4000- metre peaks in the Alps. One day I went out with the first President of the Ladies' Alpine Club, Mrs. Aubrey le Blond. She had done all the classic routes, and was fifty years old by the time she got to me. By God that woman knew what she was about! Wore breeches, she did, and a Norfolk tweed jacket. She climbed like a man, or like some man had driven her to it!

I liked being alone, though. The wind cleaned out any lingering guilt I had about my father (he died before the War, but he lived long enough to know that my future in the shop would have been doomed by the motor car), and the constant refining of my own grip on life made me feel as if independence was a battle to be won daily rather than a mantle to be inherited or a crown. The day

I did the Girdle Reverse on Lliwedd, I knew I was home. For a few hours there, I couldn't have fallen even if I had wanted to. But home was also the sudden slide when you tried to dig your toenails into the wall, the pit of panic in the gut when you tried and tried and couldn't turn a buttress, the seconds you spun in the air after letting go, held there by a piece of manila. Nothing synthetic in those days! It's what Pascal meant when he said, *'L'homme n'est qu'un roseau.'* I got that from reading to Mallory as well.

I never had any desire for anything more. Young tried to get me to go to Switzerland with him, but these were my mountains. I knew there were higher and more difficult peaks--and higher and more difficult don't always go together--but as one wag said, 'It's the first thirty feet that kill you.' Like I've told you, I was independent. I didn't like parties, political ones nor climbing ones, and I certainly didn't have the means to go about a soloing career on the continent. Perhaps if I'd been different and had gone with Young, I might have been to Everest. I don't know. And I don't really care.

It was June of 1916, I told Mallory. Our gunboat made its nightly runs with the supply ships from Folkstone to Calais. There were eight of us. Captain Hamilton was on the bridge, such as it was. The superstructures on those boats were flimsy. They were built for speed. We had a small-bore cannon on the bow and two light machine-guns, as well as our depth-charges. Each of the crew had a Lee Enfield of his own. It was dark out there. There were stars, but no moon. The moon was a killer. We navigated without running lights to the north of the convoy. An occasional signal from a lamp would cut through the black curtain. The Germans-- we called them the Hun--had U-boats that would come around Jutland and into the North Sea. They'd nip down to the Channel, do their business, and get out quick. We had no radar then, only hydrophones that could pick up sound but not locate the source unless the U-boat was stopped. It was mostly done by sight and the human ear, and at night the eyes weren't much good. We generally conceded one thump, or two at most, and then tried to time the distance of the next one. You could tell the direction of the torpedoes from where they hit. Then we'd race in and let the charges go. Sometimes we were lucky. There'd be some debris and a body or two. But mostly they got away. The main thing was to keep them from doing too much damage, getting a second ship, for example. They never did that on any runs I was on, until one night they sent out the whole damn underwater navy. Or it seemed like that. Three ships got hit at once. We went in to the fire and smoke of the nearest one. But another torpedo hit the bunkers, and they blew up in our face. I remember going up in the air, and thinking I was falling into the sky. The next thing I knew I was in the water. My shoulders and head were getting burned by the flames, so I ducked below. The Channel is like an ice-bucket, even in the summer. Don't let anyone say it isn't. And it wasn't summer. It was the beginning of June.

I swam to an overturned lifeboat and crawled on. It was one of our small ones, punched in at the stern, but still floating. There didn't seem to be anyone else about, though I could hear cries in the distance. Suddenly there was a splash nearby, and a moan. I kicked off in that direction and found him. It was Col Walker, one of the stokers. He was all of seventeen, though big and strong. That's how he'd got in the navy. It took all my strength to pull him up on the lifeboat, and we both lay there, gasping for breath. When I slowed down, and he continued to heave, I looked at him in the firelight. His face must have been pure agony. On one side, the side I hadn't seen in the water, the skin had been peeled away. No, *flayed*. I tried to push the band of his wool cap up, away from the wound. Instead it came off. He had little hair left. I could see his eyes now. They were the eyes of a boy who was terrified at how small he had become because his big, reliable body hurt so much.

We lay there together for hours, rocking in the swell, and drifting away from the wrecks. With the early light there was a mist, and I could see nothing around us. My fingers were stiff and aching from the effort of gripping the keel. I'd pulled Walker up high so he'd been resting on the boat's curve without having to hang on. But now he was sliding slowly backward. I grabbed him with one hand under his jacket, half turning on my side to do so. It was a painful position, and I couldn't keep my hold. I shook him as best I could to try and rouse him. But it was no good. His eyes opened and saw me, I'm sure, but he couldn't help himself. And so, after awhile, I just let him go. It was him or me, but I never thought of it like that then. I had no more strength in the one arm I could give to him. My other arm and hand were for the keel. They were hard and wooden like the keel. He slid away from me into the water. For a long time I watched him there, as the jacket buoyed him. Then he floated away and I never saw him again. That afternoon I was picked up by a fishing smack a few miles off Dover. I was back in another gunboat the next week.

I don't know what I expected from Mallory. Under ordinary circumstances anyone listening to me might have asked a question or two. I think I wanted some questions. I hadn't thought about Walker for a long time, and certainly hadn't told anyone the story of that night and morning in the water. I knew Mallory had heard me because he never took his eyes off me while I was talking, at least whenever I looked across at him he didn't. I felt that I hadn't had his attention so completely until then. Of course, he didn't say anything. But from that day forward, we were closer somehow. When you tell a story, you go into yourself. The person listening is only important as a listener, and you don't consider what's going on in them. It wasn't for a long while that I connected Walker to Irvine.

I don't want you to think he was my whole life. He wasn't. Not by far. I'd gotten married in '21. Bronwen from Capel Curig, she was. She had a bit of money from her family, and that's how we started this place. Didn't know that, did you? It wasn't the Llanberis Lodge back then. Teifi Inn we called it just to confuse the toffs. Bronwen took care of the meals and rooms, and I did the grounds and the climbers. Not the real ones. They went up to the Pass or Pen-y-Gwryd. It was the weekenders and holidayers we got, though once in awhile a North American would come through who'd learn to climb on the rock walls out west in Yosemite or the Rockies. I'd get a rare old talk going then.

It was difficult at first, but after a year or two we started to get some regulars. And when Gorphwysfa closed and the hotel was made into a hostel for young people, some of the older climbers came into the village at night, especially over Christmas and in the early spring. We had a boy the year after we opened. He's dead now, like his mother. Donald was in India with the RAF. He was killed over Burma in '44. I still miss him.

I never told Bronwen about Mallory. She knew about Mr. Jones alright. But just that he was an eccentric Englishman, a little older than me, who used to climb. She knew I was happy going over to him that once or twice a week for a few hours. It didn't interfere with anything at the Inn, so she was content. When Donald was about twelve I took him over to the farm. Mallory looked at me when I introduced him as my son. I hadn't talked about my family since I knew he had kids of his own, not to mention Ruth. Young and I didn't know how deeply he had buried all that, or if he had, so we didn't take any chances. But finally I thought it couldn't matter anymore. If he was thinking about his loss, he certainly wasn't doing so in any way I could recognize. It had been ten years since Everest.

'Donald, this is Mr. Jones.' The lad put out his hand. To my surprise Mallory took it. In all my years with him we'd never touched, not even accidentally. It was as if his body was sealed off, like Nepal had been, and still was, so that they had to take the north side of Everest through Tibet. He was very clean, Mallory, and always dressed smartly in the clothes that Young provided. He still smoked that damn pipe, the same one, I think, that he'd recovered from the Bowling Green ledge, but the tobacco wasn't foul, and he only did so outdoors. What I'm trying to say is that I was not put off by his appearance. Many a time I almost reached out to pat his shoulder in a gesture of exclamation, or even just to assure him about something. But I always caught myself. Everything about him said, *keep your distance, and all will be fine between us.* Even Young, after a struggle, gave up his hugs of greeting. Mallory just stood there, you see. It wasn't as if he was offended, just not interested. He allowed Young's embraces those first few times, and Young couldn't stand that. So, as I said, his taking Donald's hand was completely unexpected.

I'd told Donald about Mr. Jones's face, how he had hurt it in a fall. And that he couldn't speak because he'd lost his voice. When I first said this, Donald asked me where, and said we should help Mr. Jones find it. I said it was far away, and that when Mr. Jones wanted to find it he would. We should respect that, I said. But you know how young ones are. Donald hadn't been there two minutes when he said, "Mr. Jones, where is your voice?"

Mallory was in the middle of putting some tobacco in that pipe. At first I thought he hadn't heard, and then that he was just ignoring Donald. But after a few moments, he lowered his pipe and raised his right arm. I was shocked. He was pointing southeast, over the Pennines. I knew what was in that gesture, and it set me back on my heels, I can tell you. Young and I had not dared to bring up the past. It had become less a matter of concern and more a matter of civility as the years passed, but the integrity of what had been constructed was always on the line, along with the builders' reputations. What I had said to Donald about respect was really a self-imposed rule I had no plans to break.

Donald seemed satisfied that he knew the general direction of the voice's whereabouts and let the subject drop. It wasn't the question, but the innocence behind it, I think, that prompted the response, as if Mallory had been taken back to a moment when time, as it did yet for Donald, stood still all around him and silence was a white space that not only could be, but *ought* to be, filled with any sound he wanted to make. I only know they became fast friends for the next seven years, until Donald went off to war. And it was Donald who got him climbing again.

Mallory, you know, was forty-eight years old in 1934, and I wasn't much younger. I was still a guide, but my taste for it was flagging. Not for the climbing. It was the company that was making me tired. I hadn't given any thought to Mallory ever going up again. Whenever I'd mentioned the possibility in the first year or two, he'd just turned away. I could tell it bothered him, so I stopped. Naturally, I thought he was connecting Snowdon to Everest, and the associations were too troubling. Young agreed, so nothing more was said.

What I did like doing was climbing with Donald. We started with small trips when he was six or seven. He had no fear of heights, and it wasn't just because he was a kid who didn't know any better. He was cool on a pitch, with a wild peculiar joy that bubbled up in him only after he'd done what he was supposed to to do, and done it well. I'd always been methodical on the mountain, never in a hurry, and always as sure as I could be of the next step. I wasn't pretty to watch, but I was dependable, and usually got to where I wanted to go. Donald was more than pretty. He had a kind of polish about him, and his balance was true. I'd always felt alive up there, but I didn't know what life was until I was with him. By the time he was fourteen he was as good as anyone who'd ever been on Snowdon.

About a year after he met Mallory, I found out. Donald had been going over to the farm on weekends and sometimes after school when his chores were done at the Inn. When I'd asked him what they did together, he replied that they walked in the valley and around the lake. Mr. Jones liked the birds, especially the hawks that circled above, riding the currents of air that came down from Graig Dhu. Did I know that Mr. Jones could make rocks skip eight times on Lyn Idwal? If I'd paid attention I might have noticed the change, the brightness in Mallory's cheeks, and the way he strode ahead of me on our walks. He seemed impatient of the reading sometimes, though he was liking *The Forsyte Saga*.

'Da,' Donald said. 'You never told me he was so good on the hills.'

I was deep in a drainage ditch I was extending from the Inn to the fields, and wasn't paying much attention. 'Who's that, Donald?'

'Mr. Jones. He's not showy or nothing. But he's like a great cat on the rocks. I've never seen anyone like him for finding a grip where there is none. Why just...'

I'd dropped the shovel and was staring up at him. 'You mean you've seen him *climb*?'

'Yes, Da, what do you think I've been telling you? We went up the Great Gully...'

'*We!* You've been with him? When? How many times?'

46

He could see I was excited, but of course he didn't know why. It was all I could do to keep from running in and phoning Young without finding out more. Donald told me that one morning about three weeks before, when they'd returned from a walk, Mr. Jones hadn't gone in the front door, but instead went along the track that led to the base of the Graig behind the farm. Donald was curious because they hadn't been this way, though Mr. Jones seemed comfortable on the rough ground. They stopped at the foot of a cliff in which a fissure rose in a jagged line for a hundred feet and then gave way to a blank wall for another hundred or more. Mr. Jones looked at Donald as if to say, "Shall we, then?" And they were off. He led and Donald followed. The fissure narrowed as the cliff steepened, and not even Donald could get his smaller body in the crack and brace himself. So they went up like spiders, hands and feet alternately in the cleft, faces hugging the rock.

'He must be as old as you, Da, and I could hardly keep up with him.' He meant no insult by this. He was just used to my slower ways.

When they got to the wall, Mallory--it was Mallory I was hearing about!-- signaled Donald to wait. He placed his boots firmly against the rock bent his knee to his chest and simply glided upward. Donald watched him, in awe, I think, for the first time in his young life of what could happen between a man and a mountain. I was angry because there wasn't a rope, but astonished at what I was being told. After a decade, George Mallory was climbing again, and it seemed he had lost few of his powers! I had no illusions. He could not be the man he was once. But that he wanted to climb! That he would show this to someone else! Since that day, they had been out on Craig yr Ysfa, Clogwyn du'r Arddu, and up the Eastern Gully of Glyder Fach where his friend Robertson had died in 1910. That night I phoned Young.

'It's dangerous,' he said immediately.

'He seems as good as he ever was.'

'No, its dangerous for *us*, for what we've tried to do.' I knew what he meant, but it upset me that he wasn't thinking of Mallory.

'Maybe he's waking up. Getting over it,' I said somewhat sharply.

'Davies. George Mallory is dead. Remember that. Your son has been climbing with a Mr. Jones. Remember why we started it all.'

I wanted to remind him that I hadn't made any of the decisions that he and Norton had. That I'd only agreed to maintain what was already in place. As if anticipating me, he said, 'It's called being an accessory after the fact. The law wouldn't let you survive the scandal either.' Then, in a softer tone, 'Think of the pain it would cause if he did wake up.'

'Alright,' I said. 'But there's nothing we can do about it, is there? I don't understand what's happening any more than Donald does.'

'*They also serve who only stand and wait.*' It was Cambridge talking. But despite the certainties, there was some alarm in that voice that was telling me to think of England. Instead I thought of Mallory and Everest.

'Watch him closely. If he speaks let me know right away.'

Your guess is as good as mine. There are those who'd say that Donald was Andrew Irvine all over again. That it was a way to deal with the guilt. But I think it was Mallory all over again. When he was a master at Charterhouse he would bring certain boys to the Pass, ones like Graves, just as Graham Irving had recruited him for the Alps. He loved showing them what he knew, and they loved him for it. Look at *Goodbye to All That*. Mallory gave Graves books by Shaw, Brooke, Wells, and others, and introduced him to the editor of *Georgian Poetry*, but he did something better, Graves says, and that was to take him climbing on Snowdon in school holidays. So I think he was going back with Donald. Back to a time when it was safe--before the War where so many of those boys died, before Everest and all the politics of climbing took him over.

But it was more complicated than that too. You see, Donald could *climb*. Mallory could refine certain things Donald tried on a pitch or traverse, and he did. If Donald were here he would tell you that. But it wasn't a master-pupil situation. It was more like Mallory was climbing with himself, if you know what I mean. A younger version of himself. It worked for him because he knew he couldn't change the past--maybe that's why he was so disturbed by that fellow Gatsby. There was no pressure on him to speak to Donald, then. Donald could do all the talking because Mallory had already said the words years ago. Maybe I'm not making much sense. All I know is he seemed happy, and there was no need to take up Geoffrey Young's concerns. Meanwhile, of course, he must have been talking to himself, in preparation for writing to himself, that is. I didn't see the journal until after Donald died.

What I've just said about Mallory going back only formed itself slowly in my mind over the next few weeks and months after Donald told his tale. I still don't pretend to understand it. You've got all your specialists nowadays who'd have him opened up in an afternoon's session on the couch. Gutted's more like it. I just wanted to make sure if he was waking up there wouldn't be any sudden explosion on the mountain. What happened to Irvine was all speculation, but this was my son who was with him now. Young had written to Mallory about his taking Ruth to the Alps just before the War:

> *You are so good at what you do in the mountains that you sometimes forget others may not have your talent or commitment to climbing. They have sworn a fealty to you and would follow you anywhere, but if they slip, as they are bound to do, even your wondrous abilities may not save them or yourself.*

There was a far greater eloquence here than I could possibly summon up, but it only began to touch upon the situation in front of me. For the first time, I spoke to Mallory directly about something other than trivial things. I realize now I was taking a tremendous risk.

'I'm glad you're climbing again. But I want you to promise me that Donald's safety comes first. Whatever you're going through up there, he doesn't know who you are. Climb with him, but let him be the climber he is. Don't let anything interfere with that.' It was like stepping out on a cornice to prevent an avalanche. I stood more than a good chance of starting what I was trying to stop.

He looked at me for a few moments. Then he nodded. A simple nod of his head. But in more than a decade I hadn't had anything like it. It would have to do.

We often went together after that, he and Donald and I. We'd pack a lunch and head for the hills, two men *d'un certain age*, as the French say, and a boy who never gave time a thought, except when he had chores to do. One afternoon on the precipices of Lliwedd, he did something remarkable for a man of fifty. Oh I know Bonington went to the top of Everest at that age, or near to it, but this was different. He was by himself, only his hands and legs to support him, nothing else. And I saw him take a wall that was not meant to be taken.

We had come up by a route I had not tried before through a series of chimneys and bigger gullies to a point where the buttress narrowed to a knife-edge, and found our way blocked by a perfectly smooth piece of rock wall that hung over the void at a lethal angle and offered no hold of any kind that I could see. I never had any use for pitons and fixed ropes on Snowdon, but I soon saw that wall could only be hammered into submission, and was glad we lacked the tools. We studied it for a bit, and then I said, 'It's hopeless. We'll have to retreat.' Donald sighed. Whatever his reservoirs of optimism, he knew when he was beaten. Mallory held up his hand, motioning us to wait a moment.

In looking for a point of entry onto the wall, we had confined our vision to the surface immediately next to us and just beyond. A slight curve in the rock prevented us from seeing the details of its surface more than twenty feet away. Mallory went down from the ledge on which we stood to the perpendicular rampart that met the angle on a line roughly horizontal from our foot level. Before we knew it, he was out on the face, inching sideways like a crab until he disappeared around the curve, lost to sight and sound. A few minutes passed. We dared not call out for fear of startling him and breaking his concentration. It would have been worse if there were no reply. We strained our ears to that silence, listening for the slightest scrape of boot on rock, the smallest indication he still clung to the wall. I was looking down to the place where he had vanished, when Donald touched my sleeve and put his fingers to his lips. He motioned upwards and out with his eyes. There was Mallory coming back toward us on the angle, about thirty feet above our heads and only inches from the end of the overhang. He was clinging by the fingers of his left hand, with one foot on what must have been a tiny knob. Very slowly he pushed his right hand upward over the top of the wall and moved it along the narrow shelf. Once he pulled out a tuft of earth and grass, but there seemed nothing substantial for him to grasp. He tried again further to the right and still there was nothing. He couldn't have had much reserve in him when he crossed over his left arm and pushed off with that one foot. It must have been a leap of faith, but later Donald said no, it was a process of elimination. The right hand gripped whatever was waiting for him there. In a moment he had pulled himself up and over. The rope came down to us from above. It was the finest piece of climbing I've ever seen, and I said so when we reached him. If I had been Geoffrey Young, I would have hugged him. Donald kept shouting, 'I told you so, Da, I told you so,' until I had to hug him. Mallory coiled the rope, but he was smiling. Ah, how he was smiling.

Donald enlisted in the RAF in 1940. He'd been in the mist on Snowdon, he said, but never *above* the clouds. He did his training in Norfolk and had his wings in six months. Then they sent him off to India. He told us that if he had the chance he'd try to get to Everest, but of course everything was closed down because of the war, so we all laughed at the thought of him trekking through Japanese-infested jungles, carrying an ice-axe for a sidearm. We got letters from him, but they were censored, and so the news was quite basic. He flew reconnaissance mostly, out of Assam towards the southeast. He was in a few skirmishes, but nothing to worry about, he said. In late June, 1944, just after the D-Day landings, a letter arrived from him that was postmarked London. A mate of his had been invalided out, and Donald asked him to carry home some mail that wouldn't have passed the censors. It was addressed to me and to Mr. Jones.

He'd been to Everest, but not by the old route. He'd flown his fighter up to Purnea, accompanying several transports there. He was supposed to return with some others, but had mechanical trouble. After ground crew worked on it for a few hours, he went up to check out the engine. He knew where he was going, and had thought out how long it would take him. Purnea is less than an hour from Nepal, and once you cross that border the Himalayas are right in front of you.

I came out of some haze and there was Kangchenjunga blocking the whole sky. I was at 25,000 feet, well below its summit. Using the turbo now, I climbed westward and peaked above Makalu at almost 28,000. There ahead of me and still higher was the plume of blown snow, pointing to the east. I came around on the Tibet side and saw it all--the Rongbuk Glacier, the North Col, the ridge where Mallory and Irvine disappeared. I wanted to see the Second Step and went for a look. The down-draft was terrific, and I had to fight to keep the nose up. I opened the canopy. My oxygen mask was on, but even so my lungs felt the cold! What a place! But I got some pictures. The Step looks impassable, though there's a chink in the middle that might allow for some rock-climbing. The ridge is completely exposed, and on both sides drops away for thousands of feet. And the cornices near the summit itself look deadly. It's the size of the mountain that is so staggering. It makes Snowdon seem so small, like a child's play-hill. No wonder all those expeditions were overwhelmed. You'd have to have perfect weather and a lot of luck, and even then I don't know. The south side looks interesting. Across a huge ice-fall and then up Lohtse to a col. Chomolungma, the Mother Goddess of the World! I've also heard it called Chamolang, the Sacred One. It makes me want to try the ice. When I get back I will go the Alps, Da, and maybe take you with me!

He had some explaining to do when he returned to base. There was no flight plan for one thing, and he'd been gone for four hours! How he got himself out of it, I don't know. Just a bit of red tape, he told us. It was the last message I received from him. A month later he was dead. Shot down over Burma, according to the War Office. They never found his body.

52

We studied the pictures. The Great Couloir with the Yellow Band across its top didn't have too much snow in it. I thought of Norton there, waist deep on the covered slabs. He might have made it under these conditions. The photo of the Second Step had been snapped head on and from slightly to the right, as if by someone ascending. Donald had taken a real chance here. He couldn't have been more than a few hundred feet above and out from the edge of the mountain. It looked very rough. The summit ridge lay just beyond. I wondered what Mallory was thinking. You will say I should have asked him, but there was such a look of bewilderment on his face that I could not. And then his expression changed. And I thought I saw hope.

He wept with me when the news of Donald came. The barrier against touch was down, and we held each other for a long time in front of the fire. I had lost a son, but he too had lost a part of himself. And it was a part that he'd had to find again after so many years and who knows at what cost. 'Mallory,' I said. 'Will you go with me to the Alps.' I meant it, and from the look he gave me I like to think he understood. Maybe he did. But he was already planning his own journey.

I left him alone for much of the next two years. I was deep in my grief for Donald, and there was Bronwen to look after. She looked after me, more like. She had nursed him all those years ago, and so she nursed me. I was never very good at talking to her about Donald, even when he was alive. And I regret it now. I was always so busy being a man with other men, and I mistook her strength for aggression too often. Perhaps I sensed that if she'd climbed she would have left me behind. And that made her closer to Donald than I cared to admit.

When the war ended and the army bases closed down at Bangor, together with the aerodrome, people came back to North Wales for holidays. Business at the Inn picked up, and we were kept busy. I saw Mallory once or twice a month, and then only for brief spells. He had been taking care of himself for quite a while.

Mrs. Bergschund had retired to Bangor just before the war, possibly to brood on the appalling nature of her homeland. He seemed preoccupied as I was, and though he welcomed me with a cup of tea, and even something stronger on occasion, he didn't seem sorry to see me go. But then, except for that one day in '44, he never did, did he?

It was early June, 1946. I hadn't been over for about three weeks. I paid little attention to the absence of smoke from the farm chimney. It was a warm day, and as I wasn't in the habit of ringing him up, he may well have gone out for a walk and let the fire die down. I was whistling as I went up the walk. It was late spring, the flowers were blooming in the hills, and my memories of Donald were all of his climbing years. The door was unlocked, as usual. People hereabouts still don't bother. The house was cold, but everything seemed in its place. I noticed the picture of him and Donald that I had taken on Lliwedd, and that he always kept on the mantelpiece, was gone before I saw the package.

It was a brown paper bag done up with string. On the top, held down by the picture was a note dated June 8. *I am ready now.* The same words that he'd said to Odell over twenty years before. I sat in the chair to catch my breath. And then I remembered. June 8, 1924. The same day exactly. I tore open the package. In it were many pages of journal entries, beginning on May 1, 1924 and ending on the date of the note. He had been writing them at the farm. Where had he gone? Over the Pennines, I like to think. And after that...well, you read the journals.

I telephoned Young that night. He was beside himself, and rang off quickly to contact Norton who had retired from the army by this time and was living in the south of England. If Young was always the romantic partner, Norton was the down-to-earth one who'd been through the horrors of Hong Kong . He told Young that Mallory would do what he would do and we'd all have to bear the consequences, but he thought we wouldn't hear from him again. Young had kept him abreast of developments in Wales, so he knew all about Donald and the climbs. The journals were an interesting fact, but no he didn't want to read them. It was over. The careful preparation for his leaving indicated Mallory was intent on something, and his use of the picture of himself and Donald as the paperweight implied he would not betray what that extraordinary young man had thought of him.

When Young settled down, he started to go on about Mallory stepping into the mist that Odell had prepared for him, but Norton cut him short, saying the mist was a dark veil of deception designed to keep a world intact that had exploded at the Somme, only they hadn't known it then. If Young needed any further proof, he should look at the mushroom clouds of Hiroshima and Nagasaki, higher than any mountain.

Young wept as he told me this. I thought they were tough words, and necessary ones, but Norton's weariness and cynicism meant he could only go so far with what had happened. I knew that Mallory's world had exploded on Everest in 1924 and, like Humpty Dumpty, he had been pieced together by us all, or so we thought. He was meant to live out his life as Mr. Jones, and the two decades of silence and apparent complaisance (even with the climbs!) suggested this was the case, at least to those who wanted to believe it. But the journal entries showed the hollow heart of such belief. George Mallory had finally eluded us and reshaped the myth we had sought to control. The journal and his last words were meant to take us back and him on, I suspect, to a place where even Odell at his best could not find him."

"Here, you have this. I don't need it anymore." Davies hands a typescript to me which I hesitate to accept. After all, a version of the myth is mine as well. What is Mallory going to tell me that I don't want to hear?

"Yes," I reply, as much in affirmation of my own doubts as of the old man. When I turn to go, after thanking him, he waves up at Snowdon, the child's hill. "It's your climb, now, lad," he says.

The typescript is heavy. I have been carrying it around with me for a long time. When I first went to Llanberis there was no Davies. But his tale was waiting for me. Now that I've heard it, how do I feel about *his* Mallory, whom I didn't plan on, and who isn't in any of the books, though he might be visible in the film by Captain Noel I have yet to see at the British Film Institute? That will be another story. There is no Mallory, just versions of him. In this one Davies dances, while the members of the brotherhood are turning in their graves.

FOUR

Rongbuk Base Camp, 1 May 1924:

I can't see myself vanquished. Dear Ruth, *I can't see myself vanquished, I wrote. What did I expect her to do with such words? What did I mean by them? Who was this "myself" that "I" referred to? There were always two of us. One who climbed and one who watched. Then there was the question of defeat. Did this mean the summit and only the summit was success? Or was I larger than that, capable of finding triumph in putting the best I had against that mountain? The one I called secretly Bitch Goddess of the World. This was the third time. I wasn't going to let her win.*

The plan is simple. Bruce and Odell will establish Camp V, and from there Norton and Somervell will make an attempt without oxygen. Then Irvine and I will go up with the tanks, thirty pounds each, or close enough, but it's the only way.

I wished the first two luck, but I didn't think they would make it. There wasn't room for four up there. I knew Norton wondered why I didn't take Odell. Perhaps I should have. He is still alive. But Sandy was...Sandy was. I loved him. Not like Strachey would have. Good God! I loved him for what he was. A strong boy with such openness in his face, such trust that the world was his oyster. He hadn't been broken in any way, let alone destroyed, all those things that Lieutenant Henry

57

talks about in Hemingway's book. Davies thinks it's sentimental. Maybe. I remember those two communications men at Picardy. They looked like Henry's Aymo, very dead in the rain. Henry wrote to Catherine, and when the letters weren't enough, he quit the war and went back to her. I told Geoffrey Keynes that this trip was going to be more like war than climbing. But I also told him that I didn't expect to come back. Ruth wasn't Catherine. I was never Henry. The farewell to arms could come only after victory. I tried to tell Sandy before he died.

There is a lot of snow on the lower slopes, but things seem fairly clear higher up. Things can change so quickly. It was like this at first in '22. We are twelve miles from the foot of Everest. Irvine has been fiddling with the tanks and has managed to take four or five pounds of weight away, but the truth is it's still close to thirty pounds apiece. I've been up a nearby hill, though, and it's nothing I can't manage. We're going to summit with God on our side--or tramp there in spite of His wind. We have 150 coolies to carry loads to I and II. We'll reduce the numbers to help set up III and IV. They're a good lot. I'm determined not to let anything happen to them.

It was my fault in '22. Geoffrey said otherwise, but he wasn't there. We were crossing a snow slope on the way to the North Col. It was my first avalanche. All those times in the Alps, and I had never been near one. Nine of them were carried off and we found only two alive. Noel was just behind and almost got it all on his bloody cinema. We left them where they died, at the bottom of the ice cliffs. That's what their friends and brothers wanted. I was still dreaming about it in America. It is one thing to fall through your own carelessness. But to be carried away like that with no time to prepare, no choice, was hell. I kept sliding. It was very quiet. I suppose the pressure of the snow was so great that it created a vacuum of silence in its midst. I was underneath for a few moments, and then the rope stopped me. A dead man was on the other end. That's not what I told Ruth. I wrote to Geoffrey that I remembered Donald Robertson and the others who slept but lightly. What I meant in the letter was that they were always with me. What I really meant was they haunted me. I am such a ghost for him now. Dear Ruth I think of you in a summer frock, I said, when she had nothing on. I tried to tell her about Shelley and Mary, how she changed in his eyes when she performed her domestic duties. What was I trying to say? When he was writing poems, he wasn't with her, but she was with him all the time. Everest wrote me. Where was Ruth on the page, so beautiful when she painted china?

Base Camp, 2 May 1924

It is much warmer than it was two years ago. But my ink turns to black ice. Seventeen days to go.

You have to understand. I had to understand. We could do everything we wanted to on Snowdon in a day. We measured time in minutes, hours at the most. In the Alps things stretched out a bit. There were overnight stops, sometimes two if the weather set in. But we were on holiday there, as we were at the Pass. We had a week or a fortnight, that was all. And almost ten times out of ten we accomplished our goal. On Everest we spent days shuffling from one camp to another, carrying up supplies. Or we would not get as far as intended, and if the same thing happened to those below us, we would have to go down and a mid-way load camp came into existence. The schedule changed daily depending on the wind and snow. I never felt Snowdon or Mount Blanc were alive, let alone set against us. But the hand of Everest was malevolent, slapping at us, tripping us up, beckoning us, until that last day when it took hold of my face like a claw. She took hold of my face. For I always felt the mountain as an immense female force arrayed against the desires and abilities of men. She was Chomolungma, yes. But she was more than that. How else to explain to ourselves what we couldn't apprehend? The size of the mountain, what was always hidden there, the words you tried to speak--wanted to speak--but never quite could. Not a mere mistress or lover either. Such relation-ships were left at home. We had each other, of course, but we steered away from edges. You can't tell a man your intimate thoughts and then depend on him for your life the next day, can you? No, we left our murmurings to the slopes, admitted everything there, but it was thrown back in our mouths in spindrift pellets or blasts of breath that sucked our lungs away.

Norton is a good assault leader. He paves the *via dolorosa* between Base Camp and III with food and equipment. We eat spaghetti, sausage, ham, herrings, sardines, peas, and beans, all from cans, and bacon and nuts besides. We carry tents, cookers, many layers of clothing and bedding, crampons, axes, and the damn oxygen tanks. It all adds up to several tons. III is at 21,000 feet just under the North Col, and is the jump-off to the peak. In '22 the monsoon storms hit us on June 1, which is why we must attain the summit and get everything down from III before then.

In the end, you go with so little. A two-man tent, bags, cooker, enough food for two days, lantern, and personal equipment. I had The Spirit of Man. *I should have had* Goodbye to All That, *but I didn't know how much I was leaving behind. I told my sister I was full of hope, but Noel had it right when he said I was always ill at ease. I was thirty-eight years old. When the next pilgrimmage was organized, I might have been in on the decisions about who to send, but at forty-seven it wouldn't have been me. You go through a training period, as I did with Graham Irving; then you climb with those who are your equal or better, but who are certainly more experienced; you hit your stride in your late twenties, carving out routes of your own and taking someone younger under your wing; after that, if you're going to emerge from the clouds, you are alone in the crowd of the big expedition, your eyes set on the crown. Everest was unique. Normally the unknown mountain is conquered in one, or at the most, two seasons, and by that I mean in the course of a single year. And it isn't really unknown. People have been on it, surveying it in one form or another for years. But no one had been near Everest. At least no white man, and in those days no other kind of climber remotely existed for me. In '21 we took two months to discover the East Rongbuk Glacier, which is the entrance to the North side. I told Ruth it was like the clearing away the mythic mountain and replacing it with terra firma, but there was always one more view to be had of those incredible ridges and precipices. In the end, the only myth was the one that had suggested we could do it that first year, the RGS puffery and the waving of the flag. I was more fagged out than I had ever been in the Alps, but Everest possessed me even then. We made it to the North Col and no further. No one would have survived in the wind there for more than an hour. I told David Pye that I longed for certain parts of England, especially the pastoral banks of the Cam. I told Geoffrey part of the truth. We would have died if we'd gone any higher. What I didn't tell him was how much it galled me, the difference between the vision of myself when I first set out and the pitiful condition to which I had been reduced.*

Rongbuk Base Camp, 3 May 1924

I am anxious to move up, but the organizing of so much material and so many men holds us back. It's very windy and there's new snow above the Col. As no surface snow stays intact on Everest, footprints can disappear almost immediately. There's no trace of our presence in '22, so we start all over again without cairns to mark our former endeavours. Sandy and I must leave signs.

You discover you are the only sign. You and the one you are with. You scatter things about in your hurry, but they are meant to be picked up later. If I could have removed all my clothes and used only my bare hands I would have. Everest disrobes daily, her seven veils of deception fall about you as mist or frozen spectres of oblivion that evade your grasp. Hers is the very dance of death, and as she clasps you to her there are only tunes of glory in your ears. I want to say I had no such musical illusions, but I had. The andante of slow preparation over, Sandy would be my strong right arm to keep her at a respectable distance during the allegro, and we (if she let him go) would have her final pyramid in a scherzo of swift and merciless occupation. If it was necessary to rape Everest, I thought, then so be it, or she would not yield. Did she rape me, then, in retribution? On my knees on that final arrête? Or did she enter me in ways I could not have begun to imagine, so trained were the habits of my embrace? Dear Ruth, I said. How I long for you at night in the sleeping-bag of my desires. It was to keep her away, I spoke, but it was never any use. Her faces replaced your face. Your breasts huge slabs of rock. Your thighs cold couloirs of desire. Between your legs the place where flags are planted. You see how I could not talk of such things, though I am convinced I was not alone with such feelings. We were the first European Himalayans, and were therefore free to imagine anything we chose. Indeed, we had to imagine or else be crushed beneath the weight of so much mountain, the prospect of failure that would bring us below the level of our porters who had in comparison, we thought, so little on their minds. Even Somervell, who became a medical missionary, had his dreams.

Camp II, 4 May 1924

Got the porters involved in something besides carrying loads. Irvine and I helped them build a stone-walled *sangar* for their accomodation. We used a tent for roof cover, and the men-children were at their ease. They even gave us a song afterwards! Everything is up here now for the push to III. But clouds are coming in, and I expect we will have a rough night.

I lay there listening to the wind. The night Geoffrey and I were on the Dente Blanche there was a wind. It was his first big climb after he lost his leg. In the hut we tried to play cards with a pack of thirty-six. It was so cold we went to bed for two hours before we made dinner. Over the food, some barely warm stew and tea, we talked of an incident we'd heard about in the War. A Canadian officer released a great number of cavalry horses from a train as a kind of protest, it seems. He'd already shot his immediate commanding officer, and later killed a picket who challenged him, a private who ran up and tried to grab his bridle. No one knows where he was taking the herd, but he ended up under seige in a barn, surrounded by British troops. They set fire to it, and eventually got him out, but he was badly burned. The strange thing was that when he was asked to give himself up--and he was alone in the barn except for the horses--he replied in the plural: "No, we will not surrender," or something like that. Geoffrey said he was quite mad, which is what the court-martial determined. So he wasn't shot, but sent to a hospital in England. At the time, there was great debate as to whether he deserved to be punished. Some people thought him a hero. It came out that his commanding officer had just killed a subordinate because he would not obey an order to stand and be slaughtered amidst falling shells. Horses were there too. The Canadian and his fellow wanted to let them out of the paddock to save them, but the officer wouldn't permit it. Said it would be a traitorous act, and ordered them not to retreat. I said to Geoffrey that I wasn't always sure about the line that separates sanity and madness when I was in the trenches. Courage lay between sometimes. We spoke of Owen's poetry, especially Dulce et Decorum Est. *He was deemed to be unstable and spent some months with Sassoon and that famous doctor who studied shell shock. When he was cured he went back and was killed the week before Armistice.* Pro Patria More. Pro RGS More? *Good God, no!* Pro George Mallory More? *Was that sweet and fitting? Did I use words like* traitor *and* no retreat? *Did I speak aloud? No guns on Everest. Just axes and falling rock. When I got home from the Alps one day, Ruth lay there with a child in her arms. Our son, born ten days early and half an hour before.*

Woke to bright sunshine and a mountain scoured by the wind. We will go up to III.

Camp III, 5 May 1924
There was a tiny cairn to those porters killed in '22. The only men at the time known to have died on Everest. Little had changed, though the glacier had been shifting beneath the stones for two years. Shifting beneath me, as well, though I did not like to think of it. Dear Ruth, I said, I am the strongest. None of the others quite measure up to me. Irvine is so young and strong while I must bend with the wind. We will be perfect companions with or without the gas. But I assured myself I was the lone horse, finding the best way. It was like hallucinating when the oxygen tanks ran low. Or coming down from high places, the solitary man. I felt like that in America, though thousands turned out for me. Reggie Poel, from Cambridge days, was playing the ghost in Hamlet *on Broadway. It was a bad production, but the prince was so isolated with all that weight on his shoulders. I wanted to cross the footlights and talk with him. Someone said you could depend on Sandy Irvine for everything except conversation. It wasn't fair. That night at VI he told me everything. The next morning we put on our masks.*

The stocking of III has been a disaster. A blizzard hit the second group of porters, and although I went down to them, they wouldn't budge. So there's a dump camp below us now. It's up to me to get the supplies moving. Some of the porters are ill and vomiting. I have given them some high-altitude bags. I must take my boots to bed with me tonight to keep them from freezing.

Because it is there. Did I really say that in Philadelphia? And what did I mean? I remember telling some people when they asked WHY that there was no use to the whole venture except to obtain a summit stone for some scientists and to prove to others that man could survive at such height. I wrote an essay long ago about the mountaineer as artist, but after a certain height nothing aesthetic remains. It is a hard grind, and no pleasure about it, unless it is the closing of your eyes at the end of a day of pushing yourself and others to new limits. As for those most-quoted words, maybe they came out during my first encounter with a Tom Collins in a New York wine cellar, when a reporter was standing by. I shouldn't have said them because the sentiment was so true, and the innermost part of me revealed. Once I saw Everest in '21, the summit burned in my mind's eye like a white light. The War would have blotted it out, but it was over. There was nothing else to compare. I wanted a new vocabulary of words, and told Ruth she must help me make one. She thought I was referring to love. I was.

Camp III, 6 May 1924
I went down to the dump and got a load up here. My boots were frozen, despite the overnight arrangements, and weighed me down. I was hungry when I returned, but it was like a sleeping sickness had taken over the camp. All the porters said they were sick, and of the sahibs only Irvine and Odell were well enough to descend to carry up crucial food and extra blankets. If the sun stays out and the wind drops we can get some work done. Otherwise it is impossible.

After Virginia Stephen married Leonard Woolf, she moved in a different circle. When I met her she was at Brunswick Square with her brother Adrian and the Keynes. Maynard had been with Geoffrey to the Alps, though I didn't discover this right away. What did amaze me was that the Mr. Stephen who was the former President of the Alpine Club and the author of The Playground of Europe was Virginia's father! No one knows of the few days she and I spent together in the Lake District. We stayed in a bed and breakfast at Wasdale Head. She could have been a wonderful climber with her long legs and self-confidence, but she liked to talk. I liked it too, God knows, but not on a buttress with the rain in my eyes. We went up on Scafell once, and managed to get quite far along, though very slowly, until I had to stop and tell her it was no use. Her mind wasn't on it. And that could be fatal. We sat on a ledge beneath an overhang to shield us from the weather and she talked passionately about the Fabians. I told her somewhat ironically how enthusiastic I was, and how I had tried to no avail to convince some business men to seriously consider Fabian principles. She laughed and told me she never expected me to be an activist because I was too active at great heights already. It was a courtship of sorts, I suppose, and we were very close for that short period, though never in any way that would have compromised us had anyone discovered our identities. I read Night and Day on the way to India in '22, but nothing else until Davies read me To the Light-house. Someone, another woman novelist, I think, called her bloodless as a writer, while admitting her greatness. Well, the story of the Ramsays coursed through my veins, lover of the cold that I am. And that girl's painting! Like trying to capture Everest. The photos never do it justice in their black and white tones. They don't get close to anything or reveal the depths and angles. We should have had an artist along. Duncan Grant who did those portraits of me would have been a superb choice. He came to the Pass one Easter and did quite well on Lliwedd. He'd been to Turkey and North Africa as well and had met Matisse and Picasso. Lytton's letter to him was very silly. Something about falling in love with me. Lytton went too far on occasion and paid a pretty price. As for Virginia, I thought she would be happy with Leonard. Bloomsbury was where she wanted to be and where she shone. Ruth and I went to a gathering there one night, and she was magnifi-cent. In a long black dress, smoking like a chimney. Duncan was there with Adrian, so we talked about them both. She was very famous then, and she revelled in it. I couldn't see beneath the surface, the crevasses *below the bridge of words she had so wonderfully constructed. When Davies told me that she had drowned herself I saw us again on that Scafell ledge, on the shore before our voyage out. They had no children. Perhaps that was part of it. Mydearchildren daddy's away again two years in the War remember and then the Alps and then the biggest mountain in the world for months and months and years and years you know how much Daddy loves you and Mummy and you must be good and help her while I'm away and work hard at school and we'll go again to Westbrook and danceanddancedearruthbythetime yougetthisletterIwillbedead*

A porter told me that the monks at the Rongbuk Monastery believe we will please the demons of the mountain when we fail.

Camp II, 7 May 1924

Even though I slept well, I am unfit this morning, as are Irvine and Odell. Only Hazard seems well enough to descend to the dump and rouse the porters. They'll probably have to be pulled from their tents. I don't like to be unfair, but even though they might not be Orientals in the strict sense of the word, they do share the inertia that is particular to that race. After they have reached their limit, they just give up and refuse to move.

But what did I know of them? They were men seeking work in Darjeeling, and had never done such things at altitude before. We could not carry on any kind of extended conversation with them. Noel said it was like trying to get Irvine to talk about poetry .

Even Sandy laughed at that. The irony was that those who had been with us before, the old hands, knew about the difficulties and shifted their burden to the new recruits. But when they were roused they could carry loads of fifty to sixty pounds to Base Camp and haul our supplies above 25,000 feet. We were lucky they weren't mountaineers and lacked the sporting desire we so much cherished, or they would have been there long before us. I can't remember a single name of those who died in the avalanche in '22. Instead I remember those like myself who went too far. Humphrey Jones who did the chimney with me on Craig yr Ysfa and then with Geoffrey made a first ascent on the

Peuteret ridge in 1912. Two days later he fell with his new wife and a guide from the cliffs above that ridge. Later Geoffrey wrote me that Humphrey had been watching her instead of the single eye of the mountain. We stood in a mist at the funeral at Courmayeur with Hugh Pope. The day before Hugh had led me up a wall on the Dente Blanche in ways that showed how far he had come since the Christmas previous at the Pass. Then he had approached his climbs with too much propriety, as if it were all provender for drawing-room conversation. He had grown in the few months since I had seen him last. Perhaps too quickly. He died three weeks later on the Pic du Midi. Then there was Donald Robertson, the first to fall at Pen-y-Pass. It seems so long ago. Someone said that you could tell Donald was English by the way he carried himself, but he smiled like a Botticelli angel. None of it mattered, nor his season with us in the Alps. On the Finsteraarhorn I took off my rope while I chopped some steps on the descent. Geoffrey saw me standing there in repose, held on the face by nothing but air, and quietly told Donald to descend and fasten me again. When he slipped I whirled at the noise on a sliver of ice, but did not tumble. I could have gone then and not had any of this. When I was in Paris the next spring, I missed the annual Easter gathering at the Pass. Donald took a party up the Eastern Gully of Glyder Fach. He overreached himself on a pitch and fractured his skull. Geoffrey was there. He said the sound of Donald's head against the rock was only obliterated for him by the War. Like the sound of Sandy's head against Everest, it must echo still.

Tomorow I will go down to II and take control.

Camp II, 8 May 1924

I made an early start and to my surprise met Norton and Somervell already settled in. They weren't supposed to arrive at II until later today. We sat in the sun and discussed how best to rebuild esprit de corps among the porters. Geoff Bruce agreed to take charge of them and to get things moving between here, the dump, and III. It's good to let some of the responsibility go for awhile. I lie in the warmth of the afternoon and fall asleep. When I awake we play some picquet, this time with a proper deck. Before I left home I looked for a small, traveller's chess set, but had no luck.

It would have been a game for this mountain, though the tiny pieces would have easily been lost.

If it was a game, then perhaps only chess is analogous. We arrayed our pawns. Loaded down with our equipment, they could proceed in only one direction. Or so we thought. The mountain's pawns were the small problems. The sun in one's eyes on an ice slope, the split fingers that never closed, the need to relieve oneself at night, the boredom on stormy days. We sent out our bishops and knights, traversing at angles when necessary, but always with an eye on the royalty above. While Everest skewed us with frostbite, snowblindness, headaches, and diahorrea, and was never predictable in this. We protected our King, our human frailty and aspiration, with our assaulting Queen of determination and aggression as we established camp after camp and brought our supporting players up. Everest's Queen was the Northeast Ridge itself with its winds and clouds to obscure her final moves. Her King, of course, the summit that we tried to checkmate. Or was there perhaps no King, only an empty white board at the close, an endgame without rules?

Camp III, 9 May 1924

This was the day we were to get everything up to III and make it liveable. I started up with the first group in sunlight, but the sky turned grey and the wind heavy, and the second bunch, black dots on the glacier below, were soon obliterated. We had the Roarer Cooker which, at forty pounds, was an inordinate weight and excessive in its use of fuel. Anticipating its wonders, we struggled on with our super stove, and arrived safely just before dark. A combination of soup and stew for dinner. Delicious! And Odell, the cook for the day, had even come up with a kind of custard. Afterwards, we arranged ourselves as comfortably as we could for conversation. If we got cold, we would crawl inside our bags. To extend the evening's pleasantries, we came up with something we had never tried before. By tying back our respective tent flaps, we created a kind of large room, divided only by wind channels that occasionally blew snow in our mouths as we expounded on a variety of topics. I read several things from *The Spirit of Man.*

Everyone liked *Kubla Khan,* Odell responded to certain stanzas in *Prometheus Unbound,* and Somervell was exposed for the first time to the poetry of Emily Bronte. A very literary evening. But our dreams of poesie were interrupted in the night by colossal bursts of wind that, despite the securing of the flaps, drove in two or three inches of powdered snow. In the morning it kept up for quite a while, and we decided since we could not make any move towards the North Col for several days there must be economy at III. It was agreed that Norton, Somervell, and Odell should go for the Col first, so Irvine and I came down. The light played tricks with our eyes, and we had several tense moments.

I thought of Lockwood lost on the moors, falling in sinkholes, but somehow emerging and finding the Grange. This mountain had Heathcliff's nature, violent, intractable, bent on destruction. Or was I the one closest to him with my ambition and my ability to put everything and everyone else aside for my own purpose? But I was no misanthrope, and loved another without cruelty, or so I intended. Catherine Earnshaw did not await me at home. Ruth's time with me was more like Linton Heathcliff's sedate idea of heaven, than Catherine's wilder one, and she was true in ways the moors would not allow. In the end Heathcliff starved himself to death, held in thrall by his own vision. If I starved as well it was not because I meant to take revenge upon the world. It was Everest that crushed us until we writhed like worms beneath her foot. As for Kubla Khan, *no wonder it was so popular. Who would not have choosen Xanadu over Wuthering Heights as destination? Legend placed it somewhere in Tibet, though not on those rough plateaus we had crossed. We had declared the dome of Everest as our Paradise. Why did we not hear the "Beware, beware" of those final lines? And Coleridge hallucinating on opium, like us when the air was thin.*

Camp II, 11 May 1924

A note from Norton to say we should retire to Base Camp and recuperate for a second push. I agree. We are spent from all the hauling, and a few days in comparative civilization will do us some good.

Base Camp: tonight a champagne dinner (2 bottles) and hot baths!

We each sat there in a state of mild intoxication, glazing the surface of our shoddy appearance with our sprightly talk, grateful for a night without battering, like going back behind the lines at Picardy. But we were lulled into a false sense of security because in France, even at ten miles, the earth never ceased to shake from the distant conflict. The peace of Base Camp was deceptive, with a panorama of Everest and her sister peaks at the head of the valley dear geoffrey dear mother dear ruth having a wonderful time wish you were here love george

Base Camp May 15 1924

Went to the Rongbuk Monastery for a blessing and heard more about the demons. Perhaps there's something in it. One of the Gurkhas commanding the porters has died of a cerebral haemorrhage. One porter has severe frostbite, and another a broken leg. They believe it is because we have trespassed.

In '21 we took the Lama brocade and the monks some Homberg hats. After that, how do you take such warnings seriously. I turned a prayer wheel and listened to the chimes in the wind. It all seemed so simple, and the life we had chosen not so far removed. We had our superstitions too. Norton would not take off his leather motorcycle helmet beyond a certain height. Noel said, "Gentlemen, please" before snapping every photograph he took of us. We used to joke that we could hear him through his telephoto lens when we'd left him far below. Odell kept a certain piece of rope until it frayed and we told him we wouldn't use it any more. He then put it safely away in his rucksack. And Sandy carried that ice-axe everywhere. His 'mistress' we called it to make him blush, and asked him about those three notches. Finally I took it from him.

Base Camp, 17 May 1924

This was the planned summit day. How naive we were. We move back up in an hour or so. In III again in two more days. We have yet to taste the North Col.

70

Camp III, North Col, 20 May 1924

Norton, Odell, and I, together with a porter, made a new route to the Col. We stayed away from the terraces where the accident occured two years ago. I did most of the cutting above an ice wall and was worn out after that. Odell took over when we went above IV to the Col itself and did a splendid job leading us through the snow ridges and concealed crevasses. Norton stayed behind and put in some pickets for a fixed rope to help the others up the ice-step ladder. He didn't want us to rest at IV any longer than necessary, but it was late afternoon before we set off. We took the 1922 route back, and whether by fatigue or carelessness we had a few slips and tumbles. Norton slid a long way down out of control. Our porter's reef knot came open and it was lucky that he landed in a large patch of soft snow. And I, stupid oaf, fell into a crevasse. I saw it, of course, and prodded the overhanging snow with my axe. It looked as if it would hold, but it did not. I went down about ten feet quite fast and was saved only by my axe somehow catching between the walls. I yelled for help, but as I had been ahead of the group, marking the way, they hadn't seen me go in. I did eventually manage to climb out on the far side of the gap, and followed the others into III.

It was a ragged black hole I looked into. I was never closer to the end until the last day. On Snowdon you cannot disappear from the earth's face like that. In the Alps the other side seems just an axe-length away. On Everest it is size that kills you, the vastness of the dark. The sky above me was a sublime, blue heart of evasion, the promise of my release, and I crept toward it like a penitent, using every inch of my body in prayer. I could feel the snowflakes on my lashes, the contours of the ice I pressed against, the whole pulse of that mountain beating in my veins as I breathed its shrouded air. But it was never where I was meant to die, enclosed in a tomb Lord Carnarvon could not find. Shelley knew: Black, wintry, dead, unmeasured; without herb,/ Insect, or beast, or shape or sound of life... *If Everest was to take me, she would find me in the open, and in the open I would lie. Her wind blowing through my teeth, my gaze upon her lost horizon. When I emerged I looked her in the eye and and shook my head. We were not finished yet.*

Tonight I am coughing badly, as if my insides would come up. I start a letter to Geoffrey and tell him about the crevasse. In retrospect it seems a technical problem entirely, one I had been trained to solve. I am sure now I instinctively jammed my axe sideways to stop the fall, and then it was just a matter of measuring the predicament. But it used up a lot of strength that I must regain quickly if I am to be in on the summit push.

Camp III, 24 May 1924

A terrible time! Irvine, Somervell, and Hazard, with twelve porters, went up to IV in a light snow on the morning of the 21st. Hazard stayed there with them to wait for Odell and Bruce who were to establish V above 25,000 feet. But the snow didn't let up for two days. Hazard finally came down, but with only eight porters. The others were still at IV, badly done in and frostbitten as well. There was nothing for it but to go and get them. Norton was determined there would be no loss of life on this trip, so he, Somervell and I started out, stumbling and coughing for three hours, but eventually reaching IV. We had left Geoff Bruce behind, the most fit of us all, because if something untoward happened his knowledge of Tibet would get the expedition home. We had to carry the porters most of the way. On a traverse of some 200 feet we fixed a rope, and with Somervell at the top end and me at the other, the four men began to come along it, hand over hand. Two of them slipped and fell, rolling to a halt below. Somervell was very cool, and only his prodigious strength saved the day. He lowered himself down to the end of the rope and, as I told him later, pulled the men to himself like a biblical patriarch. Odell had hot soup waiting. It was a triumph, but what a price has been paid. I told Ruth that it was a bad time altogether and that our hopes were waning. We must get down to Camp I, at least, if we are to have any chance of recovery.

I knew it was slipping away from me. And part of me was willing to let it go. There was my position at Cambridge in University Extension to return to, a "label," as Geoffrey called it. I enjoyed the travelling, and working with young men and women who wished to better themselves. Ruth and I lived with the children in Herschel House for only four months before Everest came up. I was put on the Selection Committee. I still am not sure whether this was designed to keep me out or in. There were some who blamed me for the accident with the porters in '22, and others who questioned my leadership abilities. But Hinks at RGS put the pressure on me, and when the university gave me a six-month leave at half-pay, how could I refuse? Of course I could have refused. I told the Americans that Younghusband's emphasis on stimulating the spirit of adventure throughout the English-speaking world supplied the justification but not the motive. I said that although I loved a record deeply, I would not sacrifice myself for one, that climbing didn't balance against the serious work of everyday life. And they caught me going hand over hand up the underside of a fire escape in New York! I told them about the mountaineer as artist and quoted Matthew Arnold to them: "And glorious there, without a sound,/Across the glimmering lake,/High in the Valais depth profound,/I saw the morning break." But I knew that above the North Col it was not artistry, just sheer strength and willpower that counted. Ruth was willing, I told my father. She never owned me, and never wanted to. But really, what choice did I give her and the children? To make up I helped her paper the dining-room and put up a new fence around the tennis court. Dearest one, I told her, you are my practical guide in this life, and lead me home when I lose my way. When someone shouted out to me at a lecture, "How thrilled you must be to be going out again," I answered, "You know, I am leaving my family behind." It was fifty to one against, and I knew it. But I would die trying.

Camp I, 28 May 1924

Norton, as usual, made the right decision about our all going down. We are only now recovering from the ordeal after four days. It is to be a simpler, quicker plan. The next trek up the glacier will be the last, for better or worse. We will have two assault teams, Bruce and I, and Norton and Somervell. No oxygen. That is a mistake, I feel. We are played out, except for Bruce, and it means Irvine's expertise is no longer required. He told me he how fit he felt and that the support role wasn't his choice.

My heart ached for him. For the first time, I let him go. How old I felt as Bruce and I trudged away, abandoning my youth.

Camp IV, 2nd June, 1924

It's all over. Bruce and I left Camp I two days ago with nine porters. We reached IV the next afternoon. Yesterday started for V. The wind was the worst yet, blowing us off our track continually. At 25,000 feet five porters gave up. Bruce and I and the remainder went 300 feet higher and scraped out two small platforms for the night. We had one tent and the porters had the other. A miserable night, with snow getting in no matter what our efforts to seal things tight. In the morning no threats could budge them. I have never been so frustrated on Everest in my life. But we had no choice. We could not establish VI without them. I levelled out a third platform for Norton and Somervell, and we descended. We passed them on the way and gave them thumbs up. I shan't feel the slightest bit jealous of any success they may have.

I had to try again. The attempt with Bruce was forestalled, and I was determined not to depend on the porters again above V. I also knew how fatigued I was despite my anger at them. It turned out that Bruce had strained his heart and had to go down immediately. Oxygen was the only answer. I couldn't see Norton and Somervell succeeding, though I recognized their great strengths and abilities. But the altitude was crippling, and Norton was determined to try the Great Couloir. It seemed so indirect to me. A great deal of traversing on those slippery slabs, and after hours of effort they would still be under the Second Step. I was right. It took them almost six hours to reach the edge of the Couloir at 28,000 feet, and by then Somervell was finished. His coughing was violent, and later he almost choked to death from something lodged in his throat. Norton made a valiant effort alone, but he had to stop about 200 feet beneath the summit ridge. He was up to the waist in powdery snow with the Rongbuk Glacier almost two miles below. It was a record height, but not the record height I said I would not die for. What if they had made it? I was very polite at the time. But I know now. It would have crushed me. I had to be first or not at all. If someone had succeeded on a later expedition I could have accepted it. But then, in June 1924, I was sure it was meant to be me. There were others who were my equal technically. Odell certainly was. But no one had my vision of the crest. Only Sandy remotely understood it. I wanted him there for that. I couldn't say this to Norton, but emphasized his skill with the apparatus, and Teddy's respect for me won through, perhaps over his better judgement. After all, we had come up from III in a little under three hours, and it was the first time I had used oxygen beyond practice climbs. Odell thought that Sandy's throat was made raw through the effort, but I think he was secretly chagrined I hadn't chosen him. As I lay there that night I thought only of the mountain, tracing the steps I would take along the ridge into the unknown, and how it would soon be over. Only the weather could beat us, and that would have nothing to do with me. I had forced an endgame from Everest, and I thought the board was mine.

Dear Davies: I have brought you this far, and there are things I have to say before the final chapter. I woke up when you brought me Donald. And for this I have been always grateful. It was slow at first, but his innocence led me on. Before that I heard you through a mist, as if everything you said was filtered through a time and space I could not understand. You were very patient. I could only look away when you came too close and the mist suddenly opened to reveal a world I was not ready to assess. The books you read kept one foot on some vaguely familiar ground while with the other I wandered over the terrain Geoffrey and Teddy had discovered and you were helping to maintain. There have been many things to deal with. But first and foremost for me has been the question of my complicity. Oh, not in the myth that has been woven about my supposed exploits. I mean my complicity in my own creation of Everest as antagonist that allowed me to leave what I said I held most dear and to go where I should not have gone. I took Sandy there with me, and that is what brought me closest to the madness that you all thought you saw, but to which ironically my last reserves of will would not let me submit. In writing these journal notes I have exorcised nothing, but have embraced the demon of myself like a lost child and found the courage, so different from will, to relive that decisive night and day. After such knowledge, what forgiveness? that man Eliot said out of the wasteland of his own mind.

At the Pass, I sensed the hills were there, but they were like the Snowdon of *The Prelude*, something I had read but never visited. Until I heard Donald speak of them, the azure tints of Lyn Idwal meant more to me, though I could not say why. At first I did not understand what he meant when he spoke of climbing. My body and my mind had come apart in those ultimate hours on the Northeast Ridge, and the black hole into which I had plunged earlier on Everest was nothing compared to the chasm from which Donald delivered me. The extraordinary reunion between what I could do and what I thought I could do began early one morning at the foot of the craig behind the farm, though it took Donald's trip to Everest and his death to be completed. There was no wind, no ice, and the sun was not yet high enough to reflect from the rocks. I thought he said, "Come with me, Mr. Jones." And I did. My hands and feet found holds of their own accord. I seemd to glide through the air an inch from the cliff face, and Donald glided behind me. We rose with the sun into the sky. I wanted more of this, I knew, and in subsequent climbs my thirst was quenched daily.

Lliwedd was pure joy of movement, and slowly the better memories of it and other slopes emerged. Slowly I learned not to repress the bad ones, but years were passing. Geoffrey was so concerned I would talk, and you were waiting for me to do so. I could feel you gently push your words towards my lips and leave them their expectantly. But it was the silence I had waited for all my life that possessed me. I had always talked too much, at first to cover my reticence before the Cambridge crowd, and then on Everest to make sure I got my way. I had no need to confess, and what I give you now is no confession, but an attempted expiation for Sandy's death, which I could have prevented, and for Donald's, which I could not. These words are intended as a way on, not a way back, and every one of them has been carved from my afterlife as no ice-step was ever shaped in the time before. You will do with them as you see fit, and the world will know what you desire. I ask you only to wait until there is no one left but yourself, and to leave appropriate instructions if this is not possible. Geoffrey will be the second. He is seventy now. Odell is the youngest of us all, and may take some outlasting. But I have a strong feeling you will sit beneath Snowdon fifty years after I have gone.

Yours ever,
George Mallory

Mallory was right. Norton died in 1954, and Geoffrey Young a few years later. Hazard and Somervell had a decade or more after that. Odell lived until 1987, answering questions to the end about where exactly he saw the two black dots before the clouds came in. I do not know if I want to read Mallory's final journal entries. How will they shape my desires? Did I choose Davies, or has he chosen me? And do I understand the process? But I know I will read them. As Davies told me, it's my climb, too. I initiated everything didn't I, and so I must follow the story of the ascent to its last moment. And I must then be very careful on the way down.

FIVE

I go to see Madeleine Carroll on her farm outside Paris. It is almost sixty years since she portrayed Ruth Mallory in *The Last Climb*. Robert Donat was Mallory. It was an immensely popular film at the time, but has not been released on video, so I have never seen it. But Madeleine Carroll knew Ruth Mallory, and I am curious not only about the cinematic role she played, but also her relationship with a woman all the books on Mallory treat as a beauty and little else.

The farm is hardly that. More a country estate with horses, it is set in some low hills with a view of the Seine. Following my letter of inquiry, I received an invitation to visit. *Dear Sir,* she wrote in a small, neat hand, *I should be happy to speak with you about the making of the film. As to Ruth Mallory, we shall have to see.* I have watched Madeleine Carroll in only two films. One is the most celebrated of her career, John Buchan's *The 39 Steps,* in which Donat also co-starred. It established Alfred Hitchcock's international reputation. The other is of more personal, historical interest. *The North West Mounted Police,* with Gary Cooper, was one of that spate of Hollywood productions about the Mounties that had already reached their questionable zenith in 1936 with Nelson Eddy crooning to Jeannette MacDonald in *Rose Marie,* and would certainly touch bottom with Alan Ladd in *Saskatchewan* in the mid-fifties. I remember viewing Buchan's thriller on the late show and being stunned by Carroll's blonde beauty. I didn't know who she was, and had to look her up in a film encyclopedia. It was 1981, and she was seventy-five years old. She made her last film in 1949, retiring early rather than turn into the aging *femme fatale* like Joan Crawford or make horror films like Bette Davis.

The woman I meet is now very old. She is simply but elegantly dressed in a white linen suit buttoned close at her throat. She does not wear a wig, and her thin gray hair is curled slightly at the nape of her neck. As tea is served, I try to picture her with Davies on the lawn of the Llanberis Lodge. After we have talked for awhile, it is not too great an imaginative leap.

"We shot that film in just over a month, which was very quick, even in those days."

"Where did you do the exteriors," I ask. "Obviously the Himalayas weren't available."

"Oh, no." She laughs. "In fact we didn't even get outdoors. Everything was done in a London studio, and they added mountain footage later on. Robert and the rest of them climbed a wall with a great white sheet hung down. They were never more than five or six feet off the floor."

"Do you remember who wrote the screenplay?"

"Yes, it was Darwin Robson. He later went to Hollywood, and then was blacklisted by McCarthy." She pauses for a moment, and I wonder if she is thinking of Sterling Hayden, her second husband, who named several Hollywood personalities as fellow Communists before the House UnAmerican Activities Committee in 1951. "He was restricted, you know, by the portrait of Mallory that the public wanted. The romantic hero on a magnificent quest who dies a magnificent death. As for the things I had to say as Ruth, well..."

I'm worried she'll pull back on this, if pushed, so I ask her if she recalls the whole Everest saga and Mallory's death.

"Of course, of course. I was still in school. Birmingham University, studying French. It didn't help me much. Do you know what I did before I went on stage? Modelled hats!"

I look surprised, as I am supposed to do, though the film encyclopedia has provided this bit of trivia, along with more significant information about her post-war work with UNESCO.

"It was 1924, wasn't it? When he died? Those expeditions were front-page news. My father used to read the reports from the first two out loud at the breakfast table. It was terribly thrilling to my sister and I as schoolgirls. Brave Englishmen against the elements, and all that. And when Mallory went to America, he really was the conquering hero. Climbed hand-over-hand up a fire escape in New York. Because it was there, no doubt!" Again she breaks into laughter, and asks if I'd like something stronger than tea. The whiskey, when it comes, is served straight up. There are ice shavings and a spoon beside my glass.

"It wasn't all nonsense. But a good part of it was. The opening scene has me as Ruth climbing in Wales with some friends. Naturally, we get in over our heads, and become stuck on a ledge. We grow more and more frightened as evening approaches, and I make a silly attempt to climb down. I slip, and am barely holding on by my fingertips when a hand appears above me and pulls me to safety. Of course, it belongs to George Mallory, who just happens to be in the neighbourhood! Everything goes on from there."

"How much of the actual climbing do they show?"

"Well, I've told you about the wall and the sheet. The film could include only one trip to the Himalayas, so they did all three expeditions at once. Mallory and his crew see Everest for the first time, and try to go up then. But I must say, Robert was very affecting in the final scenes. They built a little platform up on the wall and had them play cards in their sleeping bags while they talked of the last climb. Richard Greene played Irvine. He was very young at the time, barely out of his teens. But, then, Irvine was just a boy, wasn't he?"

"What did they have happen to them? I mean, no one knew. Or knows," I add.

"Oh, it wasn't difficult. They couldn't have them fall. They had to keep the legend intact. So Robert and Richard walk through the wall into immortality. And, yes, I do mean *through* the wall.

The special effects men tried to get them to disappear in a cloud of mist. You know the kind. Just the same as that used for the moor shots in *The Thirty-Nine Steps*. But it wouldn't stay in place and obscure them. We could see Robert's head and those two goggle eyes through it all. Then someone came up with the brilliant idea of cutting a hole in the wall and having them go through. It worked like a charm."

"And what was Ruth's character doing all this time."

"Crying, saying all the right things women were supposed to say back then, I suppose.

Some of her lines were quite silly. Things like, 'You must go, darling, but you will take my heart with you.' With others, though, Robson came close to poetry. A very romantic poetry, of course!"

"Mallory liked Shelley very much. And he could quote many passages from 18th and 19th-century works."

"Yes, it was *his* schooling. I was almost twenty years younger than Ruth, and yet we were both taught essentially the same thing as schoolgirls. Snippets of Elizabeth Barrett Browning and Christina Rossetti. Lots of suffering Hardy heroines."

Now is the time. "When did you meet Ruth?" I ask her.

"She came to the set one day. I remember we were shooting a scene in which she and George have just bought a house near Cambridge, and are talking of redecorating. Very domestic. There are children running around underfoot. I wasn't told of her visit. It's very disconcerting to have the 'real' person there whom you're trying to portray. Of course, that's a contradiction in terms, isn't it? Anyway, after Robert and I had settled on our colours for the drawing-room and had decided to fence in the tennis court, I came off the stage and was introduced to her."

"What was she like?"

"She was very beautiful, in fact. I'd read David Pye's biography of Mallory in preparation for the role. People called her Botticellian, and I think they were right. By this time she was in her late forties, but she looked ten years younger. David Pye says that until Mallory met her he had his head in the clouds, and that she brought him down to earth. It's strange, isn't it. How something as transitory as one's looks can have such a powerful effect."

I look at Madeleine Carroll and want to tell her of how she overwhelmed me when I saw her in the bedroom of the moor hotel with Donat. But so many must have told her this before. A fan's notes. She has already moved on.

"It wasn't just her looks. Those remarkable eyes of hers held secrets I'm sure Mallory never got to unlock. She was strong. But I only sensed that strength then. It wasn't until we began to talk much later that I found out what a rock she was. Not the kind you climb, either. Maybe like Everest. The kind you might aspire to subdue, if you were a man, but never can. I ended up apologizing that first day for the scene she had just witnessed and the dialogue I now found embarrassing for her sake.

'No,' she said. 'It wasn't like that. But George was important to people in ways I won't oppose. I knew when I gave my permission for the film to be made that it would be designed to sell tickets. Besides, I wouldn't want the world to have too much of a view of my private life.' I knew something of what she meant, of course. People always confuse you with the roles you play. The irony is that's what gives you your privacy."

"How much did you talk?

"We became quite good friends. She never visited the set again. But we would meet for lunch while the filming went on. And when it was all over we went to the premiere together. That was a night to remember!"

She points to the whiskey, and I pour another shot, this time over some ice. It is growing dark outside. But she tells me I am welcome to stay in the guest room. "This might be my last chance to talk about it all," she says. The whiskey is working, and I feel Davies pull up a chair beside me.

"She told me they had a pretty bad time of it in that last year. None of this 'take my heart with you' nonsense. They'd spent half of their ten years apart, she said, and Mallory himself had emphasized to David Pye that the 1922 attempt had been more like war than anything else. There'd been that terrible accident, with seven or eight of the porters killed in an avalanche. When someone, a close friend, I think, wrote to her after Mallory's death that he knew long ago it was going to happen, Ruth knew exactly what he was talking about. She had dreams, she said, about George falling, or just her wandering alone looking for him, that greatly disturbed her. But she couldn't tell him about them. It would have been bad form, for God's sake. Oh, it was alright for him to tell his male friends that he didn't see himself coming back, but for a woman to breathe any such thing was anathema. And she did climb herself, you know. Didn't get stuck on too many ledges, as far as I can tell. She knew the risks just as well as he did, yet she was supposed to keep the home fires burning and a stiff upper lip. A regular Mrs. Miniver. But of course I played her like that years before Greer Garson won the Oscar for her performance.

She never threatened to leave him, though it might have made a difference if she had. Mallory was very concerned with proper behaviour and adherence to codes. Have you read his letters to his friends, and theirs to him? Well, then, you know what I mean. They talked and talked about their relationships, but never really examined them. I read a book on Wilfred Owen not long ago. A man of Mallory's generation but so much more willing to sound his own thoughts and feelings. When I showed Sterling his poems during the war he called him a pansy. Sterling changed later on, after we separated. He began to read. He even wrote a novel not long before he died. I should have met him then.

Do you know that before he left on the last trip, Mallory sought out Captain Scott's widow, Kathleen. She'd married the younger brother, I think it was, of his best friend. Ruth received a letter of condolence from her after Mallory died, and later learned from her that Mallory had wanted to know how she had coped as the widow of a famous man. I don't expect this was quite so self-centered as it sounds. From what Ruth said, he felt terribly guilty, torn between his love for her and his attraction to Everest. There's one letter, isn't there, in which he writes from Everest that he just wants to prove himself worthy of her! Can you imagine the burden? He climbs and dies because of her! He'd already told her when he was serving in France that the only possible interference with their contentment would come from his personal aspirations, and that she must help keep him in check. At least he was honest, I suppose. But it was a no-win situation for Ruth. If she stifled those ambitions, he would have been miserable. If she catered to them, he could die. And, no, I don't think with Mallory there was any middle ground. Ah dear, I've gone on too long. Shall I have some sandwiches brought up?"

We eat them in the near-dark, and have coffee afterwards. She dozes off for a few minutes, wakes, and looks at me with a mischievous, almost sensual smile. "I *am* eighty-eight years old," she says.

"She thought he would die in the War. So many people she knew did die. And his great physical abilities could not save him there. Or worse, that he would come home like his best friend.

"Geoffrey Young."

"Yes. He lost a leg, didn't he. Apparently Mallory talked a brave show about rising above such misfortune, but Ruth knew how closely it brushed him. Like a bird of madness, she said. He would not have been able to rise above it. It would have killed him spiritually. And he would have never climbed again. As it was, of course, Geoffrey Young went climbing in Wales on many subsequent occasions, and Mallory with him. When Mallory was invalided home for a year with a damaged ankle, he was miserable. Not just because he was away from his men at the Front, but because he couldn't *move* in the same way. He would shut himself off for days at a time, and on either end of the self-imposed exile would be quite critical of Ruth

There was none of this in the film, of course. Nobody talked about such things in public in those days. Oh, you could be an unhappy wife if you were Anna Karenina, though Garbo was so damn beautiful, Anna's misery wasn't quite as palpable as it was supposed to be on screen. Do you know that she made that film the same year we did *The Last Climb*? But Bette Davis won the Oscar for a real tearjerker, very close in its sentiments to the Mallory story, and with a suitable title as well: *Dangerous*! I didn't have any illusions about my role, but it was every bit as good as Bette's, and we couldn't hold a candle to Garbo's Anna.

It was very bad when Mallory was in the States. He'd been away for several months in the fall of 1921, and then went right back to Tibet that same winter. When he agreed to go abroad to drum up support for the '24 expedition, Ruth knew he would return to Everest. So there was that unspoken between them as well. Then she'd get reports of the immense receptions he was receiving in New York and Philadelphia, and how he was the darling of the media. Oh, she heard later that he was terribly unhappy for a good part of the trip, and that some audiences were very small, but you can understand why she thought at the time he was living in another world from her entirely."

She glances at the clock by the window and says, "It's getting late. Why don't we continue in the morning?"

In my room, I finish my whiskey, and hear the voice of Ruth Mallory speaking to me through Madeleine Carroll. "This is as close as I will get," I say aloud. But there is another voice in the room, slightly slurred by the whiskey. "Remember, boyo," he says, "it's only a story."

The next morning, after coffee and croissants, she surprises me by asking what I know and what I'm after. I like her very much, and whatever the whiskey voice was saying, I like her story too. So I tell her about my dreams, and to my own amazement, I find myself talking to her about Davies. She listens to the entire tale, including my speculations about the journals. When I have finished I am a bit breathless. To be frank, I feel unmanned, as if I have betrayed a male circle of comrades that includes Young and Norton, as well as Davies. I stammer a little and add this coda of feelings, much to her amusement. And, as I discover, her approval.

"You know," she says, "While I was listening to you, I thought here is another myth-maker of the men-without-women party. Oh, the fact that you're here talking to me and interested in Ruth certainly alleviated that response. But it wasn't until you were honest enough just a moment ago to admit your concern about disclosure that I ceased to worry. Who do you think will be outraged with Davies' story should you decide to tell it? Why all the men who perpetrated the Mallory myth in the first place, if any

85

of them are still alive, and those old boys everywhere who continue to support it. Women won't be threatened by what you have to say. And I'll tell you I don't think even Ruth would have been threatened by it as a *story*, recognizing it as she would have for a variation on a theme.

I was in the MGM commissary when Spencer Tracy crowned Clark Gable as 'The King.' Dear Clark, he was in a way that kind of a figure. At least for awhile. But he couldn't keep it up. And I don't mean with the women in his life! He just got old, and the only way he could face the image was through drink. I don't know what would have happened to George Mallory if he had lived. If he hadn't climbed Everest then perhaps he would have had a chance to settle down with Ruth, though she worried about his ability to accept such failure, on the mountain, I mean. But had he triumphed, he would have been crowned King, and would have had to live with *that* for the rest of his life. He was an intelligent man, but he wasn't brilliant like his friends Keynes and Graves, so he wasn't going to make his mark except by climbing. Remember Houseman's "To An Athlete Dying Young"? Well, I think the aging athlete, like some aging movie stars, dies a little each day. How long could he have continued? Your friend Davies suggests he was climbing well into his fifties. That's about as long as any male lead can stay on top. Gable did it until he was two months short of sixty, and the effort killed him. For female stars it comes much earlier. Why do you think I got out when I did? Bette and Joan went on and on, but what a price they paid! Garbo was even smarter than I was. She was only six months older than me, but got out eight years sooner. From what we've told one another, you have a choice between Robert's portrayal of Mallory in *The Last Climb* and the figure you have described to me living in Wales and at last attempting to come to terms with who he was and what he had done. Again, I don't think there's any in between."

"And what about your life since you retired? I know you worked for UNESCO, but there's been no biography that I've heard of to fill in the details."

"Nor will there be. And I refuse to be a part of your story except as a relayer of Ruth Mallory's point of view. I don't pretend to understand her completely as far as her relationship with Mallory is concerned, but I don't think too many people outside of her family have tried to understand, and it must be very difficult for the family members to be objective."

"A French philosopher once said that every theory is a fragment of autobiography."

"I think he was giving too much credit to theory. Let me tell you about another scene in the film, one that I think was more complex than those involved saw at the time (and I include myself!). We actually went on location for this one, up to Mobberly in Cheshire, where Mallory was born. Robert and I walked, in character, in the church graveyard. The same church where Mallory's father had been rector and where there is a stained-glass memorial to Mallory. It was there then, and we kept away from that side of the church. Ruth and Mallory are supposed to be visiting family-- the Mallorys had long since moved to Birkenhead--and they go for a walk arm-in-arm amongst the headstones, now and again stopping to read epitaphs. It is February 1924. We were supposed to wander around and stop and look down at any headstone and say our lines. A shot of a made-up stone with some appropriate words was to be inserted, something from *Ecclesiastes*, I think, about the parting of the ways. But Robert suddenly brought us up short in front of a grave and called excitedly to the director, Terrence Rodwell. I couldn't understand why he had stopped and what was so significant about this seemingly inconsequential granite slab before us. Until I looked closely and saw the etching of the mountain. Under it were three words: *None Higher Now*. The date, I will always remember, was 1787. Of course, everyone thought it was marvellous, and we shot the scene right there, the last one between Ruth and Mallory in the film, though the camera returns to the tombstone when Robert and his companion walk through the wall at the close.

I wasn't very ironically inclined in those days, at least not deeply so, as I tend to be now. But, when I met Ruth I became aware of the gap between the man in her life and the one I'd encountered in my screen role as her. So I read that epitaph as a comment not on the climber in the hands of God, but on Everest itself still inviolate after the best--and worst--Mallory had to give. When I said this to Ruth after the premiere, she didn't reply at first. But later she told me that George was aware of the tombstone, and that she felt he had in one way or another appropriated the epitaph for his own motto. She certainly believed George was in God's heaven, but there was an ironic twist to his ascent that had somewhat altered her faith in things unequivocal."

"What happened to her? From what you are saying, she must have remained faithful to the cause in some way, but not entirely a prisoner of it."

"Yes, you're right. She raised the children away from the public eye as much as possible. It was hard in the thirties with those other expeditions going out to Tibet. And when they discovered the ice-axe the reporters were relentless. 'How did she feel?' 'What did she want done with the axe?' One fool even asked her if she wanted his body found! I thought she held up remarkably well under the strain. Then she did something very strange. At least I thought so at the time. I'm not so sure now."

"What was that?"

"She married Will Arnold-Forster, who was a member of the old climbing group."

My face must register the shock, because she asks me immediately, "Whatever is the matter?"

"Well, it's just that Will was another protégé of Geoffrey Young. Young lived with him for a while in Italy just before the War, and Mallory met him there when he was travelling with Ruth and her family before the marriage. Apparently it was to Will he first confessed his love for Ruth. I guess I'm surprised at the incredible incestuousness of it all--Kathleen Scott marries Geoffrey Young's brother, and now this. Sorry, it's probably too strong a word."

"Perhaps not, though I'm sure there's a more genteel term. Ruth moved within a very small and protective circle of friends. And she must have been quite an intimidating figure to anyone outside the circle. Can you imagine marrying Mallory's widow! I thought she was making a mistake, though, and needed to put some distance between herself and those who hallowed Mallory like a saint. But you can't always choose the perfect partner. Look at me, for heaven's sake! I had a delegation of Hollywood sisters come to me before I married Sterling. They were full of solicitous advice. 'He's ten years younger, he's wild, it won't last.' They were right, of course. But for two or three years I was never happier in my life. No, looking back on it, I think Ruth did what she had to do. She could never love anyone else the way she loved Mallory. He would have approved of her choice, and she knew that. Besides, she was still a young woman. To me now, forty-five or so is still the bloom of youth. I was filming in California and couldn't attend the wedding, but she sent me some photos and wrote me a letter while she was on her honeymoon. I went looking for it last night. Would you like to read it?"

"Yes," I say, taking the envelope from her. It is addressed to Madeleine Carroll at 20th Century Fox Studios. In the bottom right-hand corner is a tiny inked cross. She sees me studying it.

"That was a secret code I gave to close friends. The studio would immediately forward anything with that cross on it to me on location. I could be days, even weeks, away from home, and I wanted to stay in touch with certain people."

I take out the letter. On a piece of mauve-tinted paper, I see Ruth Mallory's handwriting once again:

Dear Madeleine: Will and I were so sorry you could not have been with us. Everything went wonderfully well. It was a very simple ceremony and reception afterwards. A few close friends and family. Oh, Madeleine, you are one of the very few women I have talked to about George. Cottie Sanders is another. Geoffrey and his group hold him in such esteem, and I suppose Will is one of that group. They don't speak of him in exactly hushed tones, but the bonhomie of remembrance is always a little forced and tense, as if they are afraid of any doubt slipping in. I still love George, of course. Nothing will change that. But I have come to see that his preoccupations with Everest made us all pay dearly. It was one thing for he and I to have been apart for so much of the time, but half the life of young children is too much. Yet, the paradox is he wouldn't have been the husband and father we all so loved if he hadn't been George Mallory the mountaineer. He belonged to that infernal mountain, as he called it, and he always will. It's just that I cannot live on quite that level with him anymore. When George and I met Will in Italy, Everest had not yet entered into our imaginations. I suppose I am going back in ways not to start over but to begin anew. There is a difference, I believe. Please write. And do come and stay with us when you're next in England. All my love, Ruth.

P.S. I adored The Prisoner of Zenda. *Imagine having two Ronald Colmans!*

Madeleine Carroll watches me replace the letter in the envelope, then takes it from me.

"'To begin anew.' Do you think she was right? An aunt of hers called her the 'twice-born' just before she married Mallory. And she didn't live very long after the second marriage, you know. It was cancer." She looks out the window. "I have never been able to understand the arbitrariness of it all. And if your Mr. Davies is right, then Mallory ended up outliving her."

"I wonder if Geoffrey Young told Will," I say. "It's the web of the arbitrary that bothers me."

"Yes," she replies. "But in the end, Mallory escaped the web, did he not? That boy, Davies' son, showed him the way out."

"Sometimes I think so. But I can't be sure. Part of Mallory died on Everest with Irvine. Part of him learned to live with Donald. Whether they were the same parts, whether he was twice-born, I don't know. There's also the whole matter of the conspiracy, and what I do with the information I have."

"I'll tell you something now, despite what I said before. For me, what you have is no different from *The Last Climb*. It's just the other side of the same coin of the realm. A realm Geoffrey Young and the others were all born into and could not question. Have *you* ever doubted that Mallory should have gone to Everest?"

I do not hesitate. There is no need to. "No. The irony is that Davies' story fulfills a kind of need. It allows me to re-examine the myth and even be strongly critical of its perpetrators without ever losing the romance of the climb. I suppose that makes me a figure in the Everest landscape as well."

"Of course. And you must decide what you want from all this. Is it just a matter of exposing people who are dead, or do you believe the Mallory myth deserves such a shift in attention? I hadn't really thought about such questions when I made *The Last Climb*, at least not until I met Ruth. I did talk to Robert about his role as the young William Pitt. And much later he did a film you've probably not heard of called *The Magic Box*, in which he played William Friese-Greene, the man who invented the motion picture camera. There was a lot of controversy about him. As a young man, he went to jail for bankruptcy, and he died in the middle of a speech at a film convention sometime in the early twenties, broke and the subject of much ridicule. Do you know what Robert said? He told me that when he was acting in such roles it was the only time he felt he was trying to come to terms with the mask that we all wear and project onto others. Robert was not an arrogant man, but he said that he was sure one day someone would play a version of him on the screen. And he accepted that it would not be how he saw himself, or how his close friends and family saw him. It would be a role about his roles, the ones written for him and the ones he enacted. It's been done, of course. Kenneth More was splendid. But it was Kenneth More *as* Robert Donat. Do you know what I mean?

Once, for Ruth's sake, I would have cared deeply about her having to deal with Mallory in North Wales for years without her knowing. She would have wanted to know. And she would have looked after him. In some ways, Young and the others had no right to make such a decision about Mallory, whether they thought he had killed anyone or not. But Mallory was never just Ruth's husband and the father of their children. He was a story of much greater and more disturbing dimensions when he was alive, and he remains so today. What you have to add will alter certain perceptions and leave others perfectly intact. Just as the 'disappearance' on Everest did. Since you cannot prove anything--nor do I take it you wish to--you are simply like the other storytellers in the end. As Robert once said, 'sticks in the sand.'"

It is time to go. We both know this, but sit in the room with its view of the Seine and the white blossoms in her garden. Beyond, above the fields, the hawks soar before they fall. I stand up and thank her. "Not at all," she says. "I've enjoyed it very much." She stands up too, and I realize it is the first time I have seen her this way. She is tall, taller than I thought she would be, even with the stoop of age to her shoulders.

"We won't meet again," she says. "At least not on this side of the seventh veil." She laughs. Then she turns to the table beside her and picks up something wrapped in white tissue paper. "I would like you to have these."

I take the small parcel from her hands and open it. Inside are two pictures. One is a still of Madeleine Carroll taken on the set of *The Last Climb*. The film's title is stamped at the bottom of the photo. She is staring right at the camera, lips slightly parted as if she is about to speak. Her blond hair tumbles about her shoulders. She is twenty-nine years old. The second picture has been taken quite recently. Madeleine Carroll stands on the patio of her farmhouse in the same long dress she is wearing this morning. She looks at the lens as if it is an old friend she has not seen for a long time, but has been expecting. It is a look of welcome, and one that promises more questions than answers.

"Well," she says, "which one am I? And whom do you prefer?"

"Both," I reply. "I prefer both."

"Yes. I thought you would." She leans forward and slightly upward and kisses me on each cheek, as is the French custom. A few moments later, I look back at the house from the bottom of the drive as I pull away. The sunlight bounces off the windows, reflecting all.

Arthur Benson, Mallory's chief tutor at Magdalene College, wrote of Ruth Mallory in his diary, "She is adorable, complacent, abrupt, and pays not the least bit of attention to you. She believes she can keep up her own in conversation, but the truth is she does not stay the course." Of Mallory, at a Cambridge memorial service in 1924, he says, "There was this about him--an unmatched generosity of spirit that affected everyone who came within his sphere, and an absolute refusal, in any relationship, to trade on his rare beauty and remarkable accomplishments." It is a safe bet that the extremely attentive, chief mourner in the audience knows grandiloquence when she hears it. She is also aware of the role that repressed Victorian males like Arthur Benson still enact on the English post-War stage and the plays they attempt to direct. As for Ruth's own performance, as Madeleine Carroll implies, the stories of Mallory, before and after Everest, mean much less without it.

That is the only way I want to see it. But I have come too far.

Not long ago, a man descending from the peak of Everest came across the body of a woman kneeling in the snow. He recognized her as the wife of a famous climber who had nearly summited with him, but had slipped from the final cornice. Her hair whipped by the jet stream, her lips frozen into the semblance of a smile, she stared out at the vast snow slopes of the mountain. The man made a few mental notes of her beauty for his journal, and moved on.

SIX

Davies is dead. The last storyteller of Everest. And it has been his story hasn't it? I have checked Mallory's journal against some details of the mountain in books by those who have been there and those who haven't. There are some discrepancies, especially in terms of the topography above 27,000 feet and the times it would take to climb to certain positions. For instance, in 1993 it took Seamus Byrne over three hours to negotiate the Second Step (even with the help of a ladder) and attain the summit. Members of a Japanese expedition in 1980 spent two hours getting around the First Step, although the snow was very deep that year. Moreover, it has only been a compilation of reports from the three British expeditions of the thirties and various others much later on that has clarified the configurations of the Northeast Ridge.

In 1971, Sir Percy Wyn Harris, who as Wyn Harris was on the 1933 and 1936 British teams, dismissed any suggestion that Mallory would ever have left Irvine in order to seek glory alone, and spoke knowingly of the extreme difficulties of the Second Step. It must be noted that in 1933 Wyn Harris found Andrew Irvine's ice-axe about 250 yards east of the First Step, and thus all the theories proliferated about an accident at that site. We should also remember that Sir Percy never actually saw the Second Step close-at-hand, preoccupied as he was with the Norton route through the Great Couloir.

Davies would have loved the controversy about his Mallory journals. What he wouldn't have liked was any questioning of his own life experience, and the suggestion that he had fabricated the conspiracy. The old man I spoke to in Llanberis had a very complicated response to George Mallory. That he had climbed with him before the War I have no doubt. Davies is something of a legend around the Pass. Young guides I have spoken to recently, who are only too willing to disparage the 'old-timers' and their antiquated gear, refer to him somewhat reverentially, and shake their heads at some of the routes he pioneered on Snowdon. The story of Mallory and his pipe is a strong critique, especially Davies' insistence that in his self-absorption Mallory could be dangerous to others on the slopes. But from the beginning Davies greatly admired Mallory's abilities, and much later, of course, he entrusted his son to Mr. Jones. The records show, by the way, that Donald Davies did serve in the RAF in India and disappeared on a mission over Burma in 1944. Those records also reveal there were several flights over Everest in the thirties and forties, including one or two unauthorized ones made from bases in India, so Donald's wartime sojourn was possible.

As for his having created the story of Mr. Jones out of whole cloth, that seems more fantastic than the conspiracy itself. Leaving aside the question of *why* he would do such a thing and expose his own reputation and that of his family to ridicule, there is the *how*, parts of which are much more readily investigated. My interviews with the family of Mrs. Bergschund in Bangor indicate that she was employed during the late 1920s and much of the 1930s to provide for an English gentleman who lived on a farm outside Llanberis. The man never spoke a word to her in all the years she was there, they said. Another Englishman paid her every month and provided funds for food and household items. The famous Snowdon climber Nye Davies (it was here I learned his first name!) was a good friend of the gentleman and came to visit quite often. The gentleman never bothered her and seemed to be content, but there was something in his life, Mrs. Bergschund thought, that weighed heavily on him. She retired to Bangor in 1938 and never saw him again.

Those twenty-two years of silence between 1924 and 1946 are very convenient because they allow Davies' voice the central role as he reports Mallory-Jones' behaviour and actions, particularly his response to Donald. The whole resurrection of the climber calls up our most cynical, late-twentieth century response: hero returns to teach younger version of himself the ropes.

But there's something else I discovered, very small at first glance, which I think Davies, if he knew about it, would have thrown against all doubts about his Mallory story. It is what Mr. Peters told me in the basement of the Alpine Club as we searched for that final note Mallory left for Odell. Apparently the penultimate sentence of the original was altered. Mallory wrote, in reference to the two oxygen tanks that he and Irvine each planned to carry to the top, "...the cylinders are a bloody weight," but an invisible, worried hand changed "bloody" to "beastly." Why? Probably for the same reason Robert Scott's South Pole journal was edited to eliminate negative comments about others and about anything that undermined the perception of a gallant Englishman lost in noble pursuits. In other words, George Mallory's symbolic reputation amongst those in charge of symbols was so significant yet so fragile that an expletive uttered daily by millions of supposedly lesser men and women could seriously impair it.

It's really not so far a leap from such rewriting to that by Odell at Norton's orders and the subsequent recreation of Mallory's life. The reasons are the same: to contain an image of a man crucial to the preservation of certain English ideals that had been terribly damaged but obviously not completely destroyed by the War. If you seek to control the lives of so many people by changing one distressing word, the regulation of a George Mallory who says that he killed his fellow climber and then lapses into an unpredictable silence will likely give you no second thought.

I didn't think Mallory-Jones could have been kept entirely isolated, visible in North Wales only to Davies and his son. And after a great deal of searching, and many pints of bitter in the Llanberis pub, I did find someone still alive who had encountered young Donald Davies and Mr. Jones on Snowdon. His name was

Llwellyn, and he was in his early eighties when we met in a nursing home in Caernarvon. He had delivered the mail in and around Llanberis, including monthly letters to Mrs. Bergschund postmarked "London." But he was also something of an amateur naturalist with a particular interest in falcons. The birds nested high on certain crags, and on more than one occasion when he was after eggs or just observing the birds' flights, he would see young Donald climbing with a stranger. One day on Lliwedd, he watched them descend the Terminal Arête. They came quite close to where he was sitting, and, recognizing him, Donald stopped for a bit of a chat. He introduced the stranger, and told Llwellyn that he could not speak. He was staying on a farm out beyond the Pass. Llwellyn recalled being quite shocked by the great scars on the man's face, and also somewhat intimidated by his presence. This was no ordinary Englishman up for the weekend. How did you know he was English, I asked. Oh, you can tell, said Llwellyn. Did he remember if Mr. Jones ever received any mail? Only during the war, and that was care of Nye Davies.

So Mr. Jones existed, complete with scars and silent tongue. But was he George Mallory, or had Davies created Mallory-Jones out of his Snowdon memories and his obvious antipathy to those romantic ideals that he viewed as a political creed so promoted by Geoffrey Young and company? I tried tracking Mr. Jones alone, but it was a dead end. There were no longer any farmhouses beyond the Pass, and those who had owned them way back when were dead. There were probably not many George Mallory's in Britain between the wars, but how could I begin to narrow down the Jones' file?

There is nothing, of course, in the official lives of Geoffrey Young and Edward Norton to indicate any contact with a Mr. Jones in North Wales after 1924. Young went back to the Pass more than once, but was obviously very circumspect in any visitations he might have made. I have been through the Norton-Young letters, at least all those that are available, as well as those of Odell, Hazard, and Somervell. In any reference to Everest, they all remain true to the cause. George Mallory disappeared with Andrew Irvine into Odell's mist. "The extraordinary nature of his quest," Young said at a memorial service, "serves as a glorious example to those of us he left below." Somervell, perhaps the least sentimental of the inner circle, said that Mallory was "a man for all seasons....a very large soul." As for Norton, he referred to him as "the supreme climber," and elevated him to the status of a saint who rose above the mortifications of the flesh. But Norton, at the height of such praise, also points to possibilities of the myth's derangement, when he speaks of Mallory being obsessed with the conquest of Everest, and of him as "the most formidable opponent" the mountain has had.

Odell received the most questions through the years because of his authoritative sighting of the pair. And he alone returned to Everest fourteen years later on the final British expedition before John Hunt's triumphant one in 1953. He stood up well then, getting back nearly to the height he had officially achieved in 1924. God knows what his thoughts must have been. As for the inquiries, he survived them, but had some disturbing exchanges with seers who claimed to know "the truth" about Mallory and Irvine. One of them amplified the mythic proportions of their climb when he heard from Mallory that he and Irvine had made it to the top, and huddled there exhausted and waiting for death. It was the younger man who eventually stood up, lifted his companion to his side, and tried to walk down the ridge. There were more reports like that, but most had Mallory tumbling to his death while trying to save the inexperienced Irvine. The problem was, the telepathic climbers would publish their information in the press, and Odell would be invited to respond publicly. This meant going over and over the old ground and keeping his story straight. This pressure, and the 1933 expedition members' open declaration that Mallory and Irvine could not have climbed the Second Step as Odell had described, caused him to back off a little and allow that he was no longer sure of their exact location.

The person who gave him the most trouble was a man from the Isle of Wight who claimed he was privy through visions to a terrific altercation between the older and younger climber that had disastrous consequences at a crucial point in the ascent. *The Times* ran the story. Naturally Odell was upset, as Young must have been, by this oblique reference to what they had constructed (Norton was in Hong Kong, and would not have read about it until weeks later). Odell replied to the paper that he did not see how anyone could take such a scenario seriously, and a large number of readers wrote in to denounce the psychic, not because he claimed to have had a vision of Everest, but because he had dared malign the purity of the mountain's "fiery spirit."

That left me with the journals, looking for the original of the typescript that Davies had given me, which he told me in Llanberis he kept "hereabouts." If it existed in Mallory's handwriting, it would of course grant Davies' tale a great deal of legitimacy, if not prove it outright. After some inquiries, I wrote to the solicitor who was handling the estate. There were no living relatives he could track down, but I was welcome to come to Llanberis and look through Davies' few belongings before they were disposed of.

The present owner of the Llanberis Lodge is a tall and hefty Welshman named Thomas who has retired from high places in the Foreign Service. He shows me to the back room where Davies' lived out the last years of his life and his effects are stored. There is a magnificent view of Snowdon, though the rail track mars the face like a laceration in the April sunlight. The wheeled chair is there, together with a few pieces of clothing, a pair of old climbing boots and, surprisingly, a more recent pair that look as if they have only been used once or twice. In one corner, under the window, is a small box of papers. I sit at the wooden desk in the sunlight and begin.

The stack of letters, held together by a yellow band, is not very thick. On top are those from India from Donald to his father. RAF envelopes and the censor's hand. He talks a lot about the plane he flies, and the repetition of missions broken only by a few minutes of strafing and life-and-death sorties. There are anecdotes about his mates, and some comments on the countryside (it is here the censor is most evident), and there is one wild tale about a night on the town in Delhi. They are a young man's letters for quite a while, full of energy and a focus on what is at hand, but as he moves through the war with those same mates dying around him, Donald grows tired and looks beyond the amphitheatre of operations and orders. The flight over Everest, when it comes, is at least partially in reaction to the confinements of military life and the killing zone over Burma. Davies has replaced that extraordinary letter in the pile, and I read again the words that have new meaning for me now: *The Step looks impassable, though there's a chink in the middle that might allow for some rock-climbing.* Davies thought he saw hope in Mallory's face, but he had not yet been given the journal.

Beneath the Everest message is a second group of letters that Donald wrote to Mr. Jones. These are very different. There is hardly any mention of the war. Instead Donald talks about all the climbs they have done together in minute detail, taking them step by step up various Snowdon routes, pausing to point out a clump of grass or the sheen of dew on a rock-face, emphasizing how they might subtly alter a path to make it more interesting (a code-word for 'challenging,' I learn after a few such references). There are also a lot of queries about technique, or "tactics," as Donald says. He seems particularly concerned with what Mr. Jones would do on a familiar pitch if it were covered with ice, and more than once asks about the steps they would have to take to bivouac overnight in some precarious position. He writes each letter as if he expects answers, though there is no evidence of any reply. He neither refers to anything Mr. Jones has said in answer to his inquiries, nor chastises him for his silence. But gradually, I notice, he takes care of all the questions himself, making reference to what Jones has taught him or, building on that, creating innovative solutions to problems he has not experienced directly. It is clear he wants to go to the Alps, and that he expects Jones will go with him. It is also clear, from several references, that he is very informed about the Himalayan expeditions of the twenties and thirties. He doesn't mention Mallory, except in that one letter about the flight, but he does tell Mr. Jones that if Odell could get to 27,000 feet in 1938 an older, but fit Englishman shouldn't have any trouble reaching just over half that height, which, after all, would put him on top of Mount Blanc!

At the bottom of this pile is a grey RAF envelope with the word *Deceased* stamped in red on one side. On the reverse is Davies' name and his Llanberis residence. Inside is another, smaller envelope addressed to Donald in India. The postmark has been smudged, so the date is obscured, but the lines beneath have been printed in strong black letters that remain unblemished. The envelope has been serrated along its upper edge, obviously by Davies who has read its contents and judged them the proper conclusion to this relationship with the man whose secret he never divulged to his son. I pull out the single piece of folded paper and read the words that take my breath away. *Dear Donald--thank you for telling me about your view of Everest. It was good to see the mountain through your eyes. I would like to go there again one day.* There is no signature, but the handwriting is Mallory's, the same vertical strokes I have seen over and over in his letters to Ruth and Geoffrey Young. And for a moment I am frightened by what I think I am holding in my hand. The evidence that George Mallory did not die on Everest, the proof that Nye Davies' story is not just a fantasy that consumed an old man and has left me in limbo between fact and fiction. Young and Norton's Frankenstein revealed.

And then just as quickly I realize nothing has been verified. Even if George Mallory wrote these words, there is no way to establish that he did so in 1944 as opposed to the early twenties between the first and third Everest expeditions. The opened RAF envelope does not even confirm that the note to Donald was inside, nor that it was sent to India in the first place. Who is Donald? The reputations of Young, Norton, and the others would crush any feeble attempts I might make to tell my tale, waving my piece of paper on the steps of the RGS, having it spurned by an archivist in the Alpine Club basement. I turn the box over on the desk, and scatter the contents in disarray, looking for any kind of hold, a way up. I look for a long time before I find it, reaching out, finally, to something already within my grasp.

There is no original of the journal, just clippings about Mallory, some obviously collected before Davies met Mr. Jones, some after. The 1933 report on the discovery of the ice-axe is here, together with the press speculations on what must have occured nine years previously. There is also the front page of a London newspaper, dated May 31, 1953 which glowingly describes the triumph of Hilary and Tenzing from the south side of Everest. There are a few photographs. One of Donald as a very small climber, with a rope around his little shoulder, and a big grin as he points a finger to the sky. Another of him in uniform and what looks to be an aerodrome in the background. There is also a shot of a prepossessing young couple by a fountain, and on the back the words "Nye and Bronwen, St. David's College, 1919."

I look in vain for an image of Mallory, however grainy and out of focus, perhaps on the reverse in large letters GEORGE MALLORY-JONES, PEN-Y-PASS, 1936. The note I have laid aside as useless, a piece of fool's gold in a moraine of decreasing opportunity. I place the clippings and photos back in the box, pick up the note to place it in the stack of letters, and reread the final sentence. *I would like to go there again one day.* Something clicks. There is a sudden clearing of the atmosphere above me, and for a moment the entire summit ridge is unveiled. He has told Donald, told him who he is in the only way he knows how. Told him indeed that he loves him. And invited questions that he knows will require answers when the war is over. But just as with Irvine, it is too late. Or is it?

Mallory has come down from that distant peak of self-absorption to ground we all inhabit and explore. He has taken the sacred myth of his own ascension and bloodied it with admission and possibility. I can ask nothing more of him or what has been provided here and in his final journal entry. Quietly I wrap the yellow band around the letters. I close the box and place it in the corner. Up Snowdon's flank the toy railway climbs, bearing its inveterate load of imperial tourists. I look around this room for what I think will be the last time. "Nye Davies," I say. "Story-teller."

SEVEN

It goes something like this.

"Mallory, you're full of shit!" The words echo around the amphitheatre of peaks. They ring in Andrew Irvine's ears like fiery bells. He cannot find their source. Bells peal, he thinks, like my face in this damn sun. He is sure he is alone. Who is speaking, then? Who would say such a thing? The RGS would not stand for it, let alone the Oxford Union. The words cast shame on a living legend, the world's foremost mountaineer, and someone for whom he, Andrew Comyn Irvine, has only the greatest respect. The peaks are vaguely familiar. They look like ones he has seen on Spitsbergen, but they are higher, much higher, and surround him in a perfect circle, their glaciers cascading down in great frozen waterfalls from needle pinnacles. He is standing in a huge bowl of ice. The smoothness of it is alarming, and he does not dare take a step in his fear of a sudden fall. And then of sliding, of sliding right up the immense curve of one of those glaciers to a zenith that will skewer him against the sky. But he can move his head, turn it to the right and left to search for the speaker. He does so and feels the minute shift of a heavy weight on his back, something that now he recognizes its presence threatens to shift him from his feet, pulling him backwards and down to the ice floor and the inevitable reverse glissade. He turns his neck until it hurts and sees the cylinders, larger than any he has known, and pulsating in a way he cannot decipher until he realizes they are moving in and out with his own breath. He tries to roll them off, but cannot find any attaching straps that hold them in place. It is then he realizes he is naked, except for the tanks. Why hasn't he noticed this appalling fact before? It is because in the midst of all this frozen landscape he is not cold. Instead, he is pleasantly warm, though his extremities are noticeably cooler, especially the toes of one foot. He turns his attention to the tanks again, to his disturbed sense that they seem to be growing out of his back, when the words ring out, only louder than before. "MALLORY, YOU'RE FULL OF SHIT!" It is awful. He has to put a stop to it at once, before anyone else hears, particularly George. He stretches out a hand to arrest the sound and grasps it tightly, squeezing the echoes until they die. But his own breath is threatened. He gasps for air, reaching desperately over his shoulder with his other hand in a vain attempt to grapple with the regulator. It is terrible. If he wants to breathe he has to release the words. He starts to let go. But then he sees someone off to his right and a little ahead, as naked as himself, watching the peaks. He cannot let him hear. He won't. He is suffocating, but he hangs on. The figure ahead turns and smiles, beckoning him on. It is Mallory, signalling the ascent. He has to move. And as he tries for that first, tentative step, Andrew Irvine falls and hits the ice hard. The words fly out of his hand as he feels its grip come away from his own mouth, his breath racking his body like altitude coughing, and he is awake in the tent at VI, Mallory there beside him, their down bags tangled in the tiny space.

In the summer of 1919, Odell and his wife of a few weeks were on high ground hiking through North Wales when they heard a strange sound. Couldn't be a motor car, thought Odell. Not here. And it wasn't. Instead it was a virile young man on a motorcycle.

"Good morning," said Andrew Irvine. "Is this the way to Llanfairfechan?"

Too surprised to reply, Odell merely pointed down and to the east. The cyclist waved and disappeared from Odell's life until the spring of 1923 when he saw him again at Putney during the training runs for the Oxford-Cambridge boat race. Odell was considering men to take with him on a sledging expedition to Spitsbergen that summer. The blond-haired youth had strength, leadership qualities, and (Odell remembered Wales) an obvious love of adventure. Odell signed him up on the spot. Oxford won the race by three-quarters of a lengths.

That Easter, when George Mallory was returning from his American tour, Odell let Irvine lead him up the Great Gully of Craig yr Ysfa. It would be a long leap from there to Everest, but in between was at least one Arctic peak, and so, after reaping the benefits of Irvine's endurance and mechanical aptitude in Spitsbergen, Odell recommended him to the Selection Committee in September. He was twenty-one years old. Between his reception of the Committee's letter in October 1923 and the departure of the ship for India on February 29, 1924, Irvine learned to ski in Switzerland, crossing the Oberland glaciers alone. There is no mention of any climbing in the Alps.

When George Mallory was eight years old, his family moved from Mobberley to Birkenhead because his father had become rector in the parish of St. John the Evangelist. In 1902, when Mallory was away at Winchester, studying mathematics and living a life that was like a dream, Andrew Irvine was born in Birkenhead. Too late to have been treated as an equal in Charterhouse rooms or during those days upon Lliwedd that were, as Geoffrey Young insisted, "more than we could ever desire." Too late to have any seasoning in the Alps with Uncle George. But not too late to startle Odell and his bride and then impress the expedition leader on an Arctic island by recommending pockets for sledging suits and sleeping bags that didn't moult.

And so in the dining-room of the *California* on the way to India, there might have been the first exchange between the master and the new student.

"Irvine, what do you think of oxygen for the final assault?"

"It's the very thing, and I can greatly improve the workings of the tanks."

Six weeks later, Mallory wrote to his wife that although Odell was in charge of the gas, Irvine was the engineer who knew the apparatus and who had practically invented a new instrument. He will be an extraordinarily stout companion, said Mallory, and added with reference to Irvine's lack of experience, "I hope the terrain won't be too difficult."

Much intervened, of course, between the sentiments expressed in this April 24th letter from Shekar Dzong, four days away from the Rongbuk Monastery, and the final photo of George Mallory with his protégé taken by Odell as they left Camp IV on the morning of June 6. Everest had repulsed their best efforts. Mallory tried for the summit with Geoffrey Bruce, but without oxygen. Norton made his trip to the Great Couloir with Somervell coughing behind him. Later, Norton, snowblind in the tent at III, was puzzled by Mallory's choice of Irvine over Odell. Many have speculated. But Duncan Grant, the painter, surely the only man to have had George Mallory naked and alone with him, hit the piton on the head when he said that it was difficult to see any logic in Mallory's choice.

Those who have paid attention to Grant's comment (made very late in his life) seem to have bypassed his secondary meaning, which is that *we* can't discern such logic. If to be logical is to be integral in judgement, perhaps the irony, given the complexities of his attraction to Irvine, is that Mallory was admitting the absolute integrity of his taking with him someone or something he loved deeply. "Ghostlier demarcations, keener sounds" are possibly one result of such an idea of order on Everest. These are the words of a poet Mallory never mentions, though he was born only three years after Geoffrey Young.

Camp IV, 6 June 1924

Odell fumbles with the camera. He has on fingerless gloves, but it's a clumsy box affair belonging to Captain Noel, and as usual the temperature is low, which might explain the slight lack of focus in a photo of such importance. The importance for Odell lies not in any foreshadow falling across the snow, but in his strong feeling that Mallory will win this time. And it is of that he thinks, not of his own missed opportunity. He wants a pose. At least Noel wants one. But Mallory is always moving, picking up pieces of equipment and tossing them down again, fiddling with the oxygen tanks, walking to the edge of the camp (a few steps) and looking up, as if the weather will change in the minute or two before they set off. That it can Odell knows already, and he will have this confirmed two days hence. So finally he snaps the shutter. Apart from the lack of focus, it isn't a good picture. Noel will privately chide Odell when the initial response to the tragedy is over.

Irvine stands with his back to the camera, hands in his pockets, obviously waiting. There is a slight angle to his head, as if he is looking to his left at Mallory, but his eyes could be anywhere. The oxygen tanks he carries are huge, like rocket boosters, though he has modified their combined weight down to 25 pounds. He seems as if he could propel himself towards the top. Mallory is facing Odell, but looking at the oxygen mask he is holding, perhaps to adjust it. He already has on a leather face mask, so his expression isn't visible, but there is a certain rigidity to his body that suggests annoyance. The most noticeable part of his apparel is his cloth puttees, wound from ankle to knee. It appears a very messy camp. Dark, indiscernible objects are strewn on the ground in contrast to the white band of snow that dominates the upper half of the picture. If you take your eyes away for a few moments and then glance back, things become more distinct. They cannot speak clearly because of the face masks, but you can imagine some keener sounds.

"Make sure you leave here on the afternoon of the 8th. We want to be back by early evening." (Mallory, gasping slightly, struggling with the mask)

"Of course. Is there anything special you'd like for dinner?" (Odell, placing the camera in Noel's special bag)

"More of your sardine fry!" (Irvine, lifting his arms as high as the tanks behind will permit)

"And you'll signal if you need me?"

"Of course. Though we might surprise you and turn up at III before you're up in the morning!" (Irvine)

(Mallory) "There. Got it. Alright. Watch for us near the Second Step tomorrow morning around 8.00 o'clock." (To Irvine) "I am ready now."

All vital conversations must come to an end. But not here. Odell is left to his lonely thoughts for the next fifty-eight hours, including those in the famous five minutes on his rock crag. Mallory and Irvine walk out of his frame to the upper right, and are never heard from again by the world, except in Mallory's two brief notes from V and VI. We know they speak in these camps or when they halt for cold snacks and take off their masks. The rest is gesturing and words the other cannot hear. "Dear chap, do be careful," and "Mallory, you're full of shit." A bit of history that is often overlooked: they are accompanied from IV to V by eight porters, four of whom will go on to VI, all without oxygen and none of whom can understand English niceties or obscenities.

They move slowly and steadily, conserving their energy for the decisive push. There is little wind, so they make good time. Irvine has not been this high before, and it is still only the North Col. But tonight they will be as high as Mallory has ever been! It is difficult not to look up. The immensity does not change. The whole Northeast Ridge is exposed above them, though they see it from a sharp angle, so it is not the horizontal vastness found in photographs, but a narrow series of jagged edges extending into infinity (who's to say there is not another summit ridge beyond the one they consider final). If something fearful hovers on the borders of Irvine's mind, he cannot admit it. If he did, he would have to deal with a previously unknown concern. Not what happens if you fall, but what happens if you don't stop going up? The dark angel at Mallory's shoulder simply blows the negative into the whirlwind and interrogates relentlessly. What happens if you *stop* going up, George?

Just after noon, they pause for a lunch of tea, canned ham, and dried fruit. They sit apart from the porters, or as much apart as the mountain allows.

"What do they think of all this?" Irvine asks.

"They don't think. Not about this. Unless it's to fear that they're treading on the shoulder of a goddess."

"Is that what we're doing?"

Mallory doesn't like the question. He throws away a piece of gristle and sips some tea. Irvine assumes he will be ignored. After a few more sips, Mallory responds.

"No, it's not what we're doing. We're climbers, not acolytes of Everest or the Lama of Rongbuk. If there is a goddess she doesn't see us in the same way as she does them. She lets her wind and ice deal with us indifferently. Them," he nods at the porters, "she takes personally."

"I don't know, George. Aren't we putting ourselves above them, and so above her? Isn't it a kind of blasphemy?" Irvine doesn't know exactly where he is going with this. The ground is challenging, but quite uneven.

"We're very different from them, Sandy." Mallory's voice has changed with his use of the diminutive. It is not patronizing, but rather dreamy in tone, even if the words are distinct and Mallory's face remains clear. "For one thing, they have no urge to climb this mountain, beyond the one stimulated by rupees. You've seen them collapse as we have never done and would never do because their spirit is not in it."

Or because their Spirit is in it, thinks Irvine, but does not say.

"And for another, they cannot put into words what climbing is about. The little I understand of their language tells me their response to Everest is monosyllabic and visceral. Whereas we speak volumes and have only minor gut irritations. He laughs as does Irvine at this obvious reference to the mountain 'trots', so very problematic in the cold and with layers of clothing. "Don't misunderstand me. I do not presume to suggest this difference is qualitative. We come from two distinct cultures, that is all. 'And never the twain shall meet.' Time to push on." He flings another piece of gristle into the face of what Irvine sees increasingly as the unknown and does not want to offend.

They arrive at V in late afternoon. After they have set up the two tents on the tiny platform gouged out by Mallory and Bruce almost a week before, and had some tea, they send four porters down with a note for Odell, telling him that the weather looks hopeful. One of the departing porters grasps them each by the shoulders, and says something incomprehensible. Whatever it is, Irvine knows, his eyes are saying goodbye.

When the porters have disappeared around a serac just below the camp, they crawl into their bags and rest for an hour. Neither speaks. Irvine rubs some salve into his cracked and peeling face. The sun is a friend and an enemy, but he would rather be warm than do without the blistered skin. Mallory focuses on the climb to VI. It is better to do this now. Tonight he wants his mind to drift into sleep without concern for problems or tactics. Tomorrow he will be higher than ever before. Camp VI is 1300 vertical feet above V. It took Norton and Somervell four and a half hours without oxygen. With their gas flow set at the same rate they had used from IV to V, he and Irvine should be able to cover the same distance in half that time. His mind wants to climb further, but he pulls the rope in. They will have most of an afternoon and evening to prepare for the summit. He watches the canvas roof billow outward in the wind and snap toward him at the end of its tether.

After a while he gets out of his bag, takes two aluminum pots, and tells Irvine he is going to get some snow to melt for dinner. Irvine sits up, lights the meta burner, and opens two tins of spaghetti, one tin of condensed milk, a bag of nuts, and finds the precious tea and sugar. Each full pot of snow that Mallory brings inyields a half pot of water, and it is lukewarm tea they drink because water boils at a lower temperature than down below. The whole process consumes the better part of two hours. After they have made their tea, there is water to heat for the dishes and to fill a thermos for the next morning. They eat out of necessity, not enjoyment, munching slowly, their cracked lips pained by the dilation. Their throats, though, can't get enough of the tea. The conversation is desultory and without substance. Only when the cleaning has been done and things have been stowed away does Mallory address tomorrow's climb.

"The weather looks to be fine, so there's no need for us to rush in the morning. We'll leave by 8.00 o'clock and be settled in by noon. That will give us plenty of time to go over the equipment and the plan of attack. What do you think? Will we get the same flow from the tanks?"

Irvine recognizes that the first question leads on to the second, not back into the self-sufficient statement about departure and arrival. Mallory leads and he follows, but he is proud of his accomplishments with the oxygen gear, and knows Mallory depends on his abilities here.

"Yes, I'll get up early enough in the morning to go through it all. I took an extra mouthpiece from that defective tank I left behind yesterday. If we go up with the usual flow rate, we'll have plenty for the summit."

Irvine is right. There is no perceptible flaw in his calculations. But he and Mallory have not climbed above 27,000 feet where demands upon the heart and lungs are extraordinary. Tomorrow night they will camp at just under that height, and employ oxygen to help them sleep. The next day, the last whatever happens, they will use up the gas at an alarming rate. But for now everything seems in order. They have placed their bags so their heads are at opposite ends of the tent. Leaning on arms that soon grow numb but cannot be moved because there is no other position that will suit the purpose, they relax and play picquet.

Irvine has always been on the outside when the others have discussed literature. They have thrown quotations at him and teased him especially about his slow response to poetry. He has never dared begin any kind of literary exchange with Mallory who quotes freely from *The Spirit of Man* and many other books. But now he suddenly remembers an appropriate title from his Merton days, all those long months ago, something his tutor quoted to him before an important boat race, knowing that Irvine's mind was on the coming struggle. It is "The Card Dealer" by Rossetti. But is it the brother or the sister, damn it?

He takes a chance. "George, do you know Rossetti's poem "The Card Dealer"?

Mallory lays down a king, but looks up, surprised. "No. Dante or Christina?"

Now Irvine is confused. How does Dante enter into this? Please God Mallory doesn't ask him about *The Divine Comedy*. But he is encouraged by Mallory's question. The admission of ignorance. Another chance, steering away from the Italian. "Christina."

"Tell me about it."

This is much better than 'quote me some lines' or, even worse, 'do say it me.' But Irvine hasn't got much more than the title. "Well, the card dealer is fate who deals the cards to those who wait to know what will happen to them."

"And what does happen to them?"

Panic. No, it's a long way back to England where Mallory will be able to look it up. "Some win through, but most do not. It is a dark poem, as I recall."

"Ah, the demonic, alluring female who tempts us all."

Irvine has not thought of this. There was no such temptation at Merton, and as for Everest she does not appear to him this way. So he does not venture a reply.

"Can you remember any of it? To say aloud, I mean?"

No third chance. "I think not."

Mallory lays down the Queen of Hearts. "Sandy in Wonderland," he says. They both laugh.

Sheer plod makes plough down sillion shine Mallory thinks, as he and Irvine trudge up to VI with the four porters. Hopkins. Strange fellow that. Oxford Jesuit who turned up for dinner one night at Magdalene College. Talked about inscape with Arthur Benson. Later, I got into a bit of a tiff with him about his *mountains of the mind.* Said that true climbers went to the mountains to clear their minds, that his metaphor did a disservice to the *real* heights. When he looked at me coolly and asked if I climbed, I thought he was joking. If I fall, I said, it will have nothing to do with me.

We are up to this. Sandy was the right choice. He will get a foot in the door when we return, though he will have to learn to speak in public and explain himself more directly. I will be happy to leave it all to him. Once this is done, what else remains? Of course, Geoffrey and I will still go to the Pass, and there are a few Alpine traverses to attempt. But there will be no hurry, no need to prepare for something more. Ruth will be pleased. She has been a brick for three years now. I wasn't home three months after the first expedition before I was off on the second. Then there was America, and here I am again. My family must think life is a continual jaunt to high places. The only regret I have is that we did not succeed the last time. The weather was against us, and the snow. But with a little luck Somervell and I might have made it, and all of this would not be necessary. I am tired. What is it Arthur Benson said about climbing Everest? "An achievement. Nothing more."

Irvine catches up with him, and they rest in some rock shadows. The drop is fantastic, but not comprehensible. All the shades of white against blue cancel out the depth. If you ignore the ground at your feet, it seems as if you could step across to the Rongbuk Glacier ten thousand feet away. Irvine pries loose a small boulder with his axe, and they watch it roll to the edge of the first precipice, disappearing into what, besides themselves, only Norton and Somervell can appreciate as thin air. All things considered, there is not that much snow on the mountain. On a day like this, Norton might have gone further up the Great Couloir. But the ridge beckons, the clean, sharp line to the top. The porters stand in a group, gesturing excitedly at the summit. One of them yells out a word to the Englishmen. It is not a word they have heard before, and they acknowledge him with a dismissive wave. If they had understood, they would not have believed. The word means *bird* in their language, and more specifically, *falcon*. The allusion for Mallory, at least, would be too strong. The morning's minion is here, but surely not visible to the heathen eye. His leg muscles flutter. He inhales deeply, the very breath of God. Without the mask, Chomolungma would suck the air from His lungs.

Camp VI, 7 June 1924
Dear Ruth I will leave this letter for Odell tomorrow morning. Irvine has dozed off, and I am alone. The four remaining porters went down this afternoon, as soon as we had set up camp and brewed some tea for them. We are resting on a thin rock

platform built by Norton and Somervell four days ago. They did
their best, but it is uneven and slopes away from the face. Irvine is
beneath me and must struggle, even in sleep, to keep from rolling
off, just as I must try not to fall over on him. The tiniest pebbles
somehow thrust their way through the groundsheet and the bags
into one's back, so that we will toss and turn all night. But you
know it is where I have always wanted to be. One push away from
the top of this eternal mountain. It is strange, but in my confidence
that we will succeed tomorrow, I am somewhat afraid of the
consequences of that success. Not of what the world will say. We
will not allow the carrion crew too close to Cambridge and Herschel
House, but simply close the door on this stage in our lives and look
to our family henceforth. I have often been an absent father,
though I hope that my presence, when felt, has given a taste of
what it means to quest, to look beyond immediate environs. You
have helped in this with your unwavering support of my pursuits.
But we must soon descend from what we have built and climbed
together all these years. And it is this descent that frightens me. I
am almost thirty-eight years of age. All my skills have been honed
to a razor's edge for this supreme effort. Since those first effortless
days on Snowdon, I have been climbing higher and higher. Every
chimney and buttress a way up. Mount Blanc was so easy at
eighteen I blush to think of it. In my twenties on the Aiguille Vert
I fell asleep on a ledge for a few seconds, so assured and restful was
I in the certainty of my ascent. Everest, as you know, has been
different. To *find* a mountain and nothing more, as we did in '21,
is a sobering experience. To be within striking distance of the
summit a few months later only to watch men die is another. But I
have always been confident, given the opportunity, that I was
meant to climb this mountain. I will not speak of something so
grand as destiny, if only because the dark corollary to that is fate
(the gravity of our existence). But I know the others feel it as well.
It is why Norton was not surprised when I told him of my plan to
make the third push after he and Somervell had failed. And thus
my fear. More of us have died on the way down, as we moved
toward the familiar, the traditional atmosphere, than on our climbs
towards the heavens. And yet I must descend to you and that level

plain without margins at last. Ah, dearest, do you understand how something yearns in me to see from Everest's peak another distant pinnacle yet undiscovered in the vastness of Tibet. How coming down would be then assuaged by the promise of further acclivity. Is this folly, darling, or only the desire to stay as you have always known me? Do I think these thoughts because I am about to tear away that seventh veil that has never been removed by mortal hand, to present my card to the mother goddess of the world and dance with her who has refused all partners until now? You can be sure I will reach the summit, and that I will then turn my eyes to you and home. Guide me in my steps, beloved, to where *Overhead the tree-tops meet,/Flowers and grass spring 'neath one's feet.*

"George, what you you think of the Second Step? Can we turn it?"

They are lying in the tent at VI, dinner over, the porters gone (no gaze of farewell this time, only relief that Mallory has not asked for more). The dinner was cold, a bone of contention between them. It was Mallory's turn to cook. He set up the stove just outside the entrance for a moment while he delved into the rucksack for food. Irvine, coming round the corner of the tent with his potful of snow, did not expect any obstacle and launched the tiny bit of metal into space with the force of his stride. Mallory emerged at the sound of impact and saw it roll down the slope at a shocking rate of speed and with such finality that he could think of nothing immediate to say. But he is angry, and lets Irvine know this through his silence during the meal. So much depends on so little remaining in place. Irvine, though hardly unperturbed about the incident, is less distressed. Once he lost an oar during a crucial race and mimed the last one hundred yards to keep his teammates in crucial balance. So he tries again, aiming at a sensitive target. "There's always the Couloir." With favourable results.

"We will have to climb it. According to Norton's calculations, the Couloir is some one hundred feet below the Step, and the rock tiles in it are slanted like the pitch of a roof. Even though there was not much more snow than there is now, he sank in it to his waist. It took him an hour after he left Somervell to traverse a

115

quarter of a mile and climb less than a tenth of that in height. This was after the two of them had been on the move for over six hours from here. Don't forget, they left very early in the morning. Even if Norton had managed to get out of the Couloir to the base of the final pyramid, he would never have returned in daylight. Which means, of course, he would not have returned at all."

"I looked through Noel's telescope. It looks like a solid piece of rock about eighty feet high."

"But Norton, looking upward, could see the split in the rock, and Noel's photos confirm this. It is the chink in Everest's armour. A short rock climb that will break her. Once we surmount the Step, we are home."

Irvine wonders at this peculiar choice of words, and later writes them down in his journal that he carries in his inner breast pocket over his immaculate heart. He does not attribute them to Mallory, as indeed he has not attributed many others that he plans to use as imperishable guides on future climbs. Had the journal been found, they would have represented his own unedited thoughts to those who looked for signs beyond his physical prowess.

"We'll go with two cylinders each. It's still a bloody weight, but it's the only way."

Irvine ponders this. Two cylinders means he can check for the best tanks and regulators. He'll work on that in the morning. But it will cut things very close. If they have to stop for any period of time, or one or both of them become unreasonably fatigued, there will be a choice between the summit and getting down to IV. *Ours not to reason why.* These words spring unbidden into his mind, from a poem he can quote in its entirety but doesn't think Mallory will appreciate now.

"We should be able to turn the First Step. It's more straight-forward. If the direct approach doesn't work, Noel's photos show a sweep out from it is possible on this side. We'll get back on the ridge immediately. We're fortunate there's not more snow."

The Light Brigade won't go away. Abyss to the left of them, abyss to the right of them, yawned and sundered. How to meet such slaughter with saving grace? *Yea though I walk through the valley of the shadow,* thinks Andrew Irvine. *But thou art with me,* he whispers to George Mallory, aware of the blasphemy, but to his surprise taking comfort in it. That night in his dream, he blasphemes his saviour.

Shaken by this dream, his strength sapped by the stomach disorders that woke him twice in the night, Irvine wakes in the morning to sunlight on the tent canvas, Mallory's bag empty beside him. There is a note beneath a stone by the pole. *Dear Irvine, I hope you will understand, but I do not think I will come down from this. Please tell Norton it is my responsibility entirely. Odell should arrive in early afternoon. On no account descend alone. Yours ever, G. Mallory.*

Irvine begins to hyperventilate. More than the betrayal, it is the shame of abandonment, a shame amplified by his own betrayal of Mallory in that bowl of ice. Had he cried those terrible words aloud? Was this the reason Mallory had left him? *On no account descend alone.* If he ignores the implied direction to wait for Odell, there is nothing in the note that orders him not to go up by himself. His stomach cramps are bad. Not bothering to eat anything but a tin of cold soup and a few nuts, he moves towards the ridge. It is 9.00 a.m.

Mallory has four hours start. At least that's what the initial traces of footprints suggest, and Irvine's sense of when they were supposed to break camp together. It's a clear day, but the steep angle of the mountain and the overhanging rocks prevent him from gaining any perspective of the ridge. If he sees Mallory it will not be until he is almost upon him. Irvine breathes easily, confident in the soundness of the tanks, despite the fact that he had no time to check any of the parts. He has no illusions about catching up to Mallory. The man has no equal as a climber. But he wants to meet him coming down, to show him that he deserves to be on Everest, that he can turn the First Step alone and, if necessary, climb the Second Step unaided. Perhaps, perhaps if he does that Mallory will wait for him on his own descent while he races up the summit ridge.

Irvine feels no anger. It has always been George Mallory's mountain to do with as he sees fit. In his judgement, he could

117

better tackle the summit alone. So be it. But let him at least see that Andrew Irvine would not have held him back, and that dreams were never meant for the light of day. There is a more disturbing thought. What on earth did Mallory mean by *I do not think I will come down from this*? Surely his belief in his own powers was too strong to allow such a fatalistic declaration. Someone had once said, hadn't they, that George Mallory couldn't fall off a mountain if he wanted to. So what was it? One thing is certain, if Mallory needs any help, Irvine will provide it. Too young and untried to climb into the white space between the words, he cannot discover the hesitant affirmation in what Mallory has written, or find the love he has been given.

Around noon, Irvine encounters the First Step. Like the Second, it is simply an upward extension of the cliff face that circles the mountain immediately beneath the summit. But, unlike the Second, it can be approached more or less directly and then skirted on its north side. It is a tricky manoeuvre, especially for the uninitiated, because the narrow snow patch that extends around the first tower on a steep angle becomes a cornice on its outer edge. The wind has filled in Mallory's footprints here, so Irvine has no guide. That spirit and determination Odell first noted certainly play a part, but what pulls Andrew Irvine forward is the vision of Mallory already on the summit ridge within a few feet of the crown. He is not careless, nor in so much of a hurry that he will take chances. Slowly he leaves the firmness of the rock for the uncertain qualities of the snow, his feet, though bound in three layers of socks and thick boots, prehensile in their attunement to what lies beneath them. A north wind blows in gusts at his back, pressing him against the rock face. He is aware only of a world a few inches in front of him that he reaches for with the half-extension of his right arm and leg, the rest of his body following with an unquestioning sense of duty the leading limbs. So intent is he upon such movement, the intricacies of survival, that he does not notice his goggles fogging up. And so, in total blindness, he at last achieves what only the lord of such extremeties has done before, and that on the same morning. It has taken forty minutes to cross thirty yards of snow.

Irvine sits down when he has regained the ridge, or rather he half-leans, half-sits against the northwest shoulder of the Step and extracts a frozen biscuit from his pack. He chews methodically, caught now in the rigid embrace of all that is larger than himself, and, taking off his goggles, looks the upper face of Everest in the eye. The Col where the others wait is invisible, but the whole north gradient of the mountain drops away before him, projecting outward at this point to hide the glacier almost two miles below. His eyes follow the ridge for two hundred yards, and there are the rocks marking the cliff top of the Second Step, more than an hour's plod away. Beyond that the summit pyramid. Mallory is there somewhere amongst the boulders, heading for their rendevous. He checks the regulator, and is surprised at how much oxygen he has used. More than half a tank.

When Andrew Irvine was ten years old, his father took him to Southhampton to see the *Titanic* set sail for New York. They took the train from Birkenhead, and stayed with some relatives in Dorset. Young Sandy was a collector of White Star Line memorabilia. He had picture postcards of several ships, and when he had written to the head office requesting some information about the *Titanic*, then under construction, he had received a stickpin with the company logo outlined in gold. But that was not all. "My Dear Master Irvine," the Vice-President (really his secretary, of course) had written, "I am very pleased at your interest in what will be the largest and fastest ocean liner in the world. May I take this opportunity to invite you and your family to view the *Titanic* before she embarks on her maiden voyage in April, 1912." Enclosed with the pin was an gold-braided invitation to dockside ceremonies and a pre-embarkation tour of the ship. For seven months, Sandy Irvine was the envy of his friends, some of whom tried writing the same kind of letter he had, but received no acknowledgement from the obviously busy Vice-President.

When he and his father arrived in Southhampton they were overwhelmed by the crowds and the euphoria about the *Titanic*. One stranger on the omnibus to the port told them that the ship was the size of a mountain. Sandy could not imagine anything that

119

big. He had not even been to the Peak District, less than fifty miles south of Birkenhead. When they came around the corner of the baggage terminal, there were more people in one place than he had seen in his entire life. And above them all, rising higher and higher as he tilted his head back, was a massive wall of dark steel that looked insurmountable and left him wondering how passengers ever got on board, until he saw a nearly-horizontal gangway stretching from the lower deck to the three-storied top of the customs building.

There was no guide, and they were too late for the band-playing and speeches on the quay. They wandered on the decks with hundreds of others, indistinguishable from the passengers. Sandy was very envious of a boy his age who came on board with a rucksack on his back, holding his father's hand. He heard the man say, "If you stand right at the bow when he reach New York harbour you'll be *ne plus ultra*, the first to arrive." The first-class salon was spectacular. The chandelier glittered with a thousand tiny stones, and the lush carpets and leather chairs surpassed those he had seen in the estate house outside Chester. There were men and boys everywhere, but surprisingly few women and girls, at least on the upper decks. Once, when he leaned over a taffrail, Sandy could see a crowd of dark, foreign faces below. He was puzzled because these people seemed cut off from the major events above. They stared at the flat, harbour water as if it portended untranslatable things to come. "Steerage," his father told him. "Off to see the New World. Expecting to climb up in life. But most won't."

Just as the funnel-horn sounded to signal all ashore who were going ashore, Sandy asked his father if they could go to the bow and be *ne plus ultra*. But Mr. Irvine had no patience for such a request. "There once was a boy," he said, "who wanted to go further than anyone else. And do you know what happened to him? One day he got there, and found he didn't like it." He took his son's hand and led him across the fisssure of air to the custom-house roof.

Seven days later in Birkenhead, Sandy woke in the morning and came downstairs. His father was sitting in his garden chair, a newspaper at his feet. There were tears in his eyes as he spoke. "Don't ever be that boy at the bow," he said.

Leaning against Everest, 28,000 feet above sea-level, Andrew Irvine realizes it was the first time he had been touched by ice.

George Mallory never saw the *Titanic*. He was at the Pass with his brother Trafford for the annual Easter gathering when it went down. When fifteen hundred souls are lost you pay attention. Like everyone else he read the papers (*The Times*), and marvelled at the damage a single iceberg could do to something so large, so well-designed, so unsinkable. He knew little about the bergs, much less than Andrew Irvine would discover during his Spitsbergen voyage eleven years later. They didn't interest him because the glaciers that calved them were far below the ones he'd encountered and learned to climb. There wasn't much point to icebergs, he said to Trafford, except that they were dangerous to those foolish enough to sail amongst them. Besides, there was all that hidden part beneath the surface. Nine-tenths of the total mass, apparently. Better to stick to the ice you could be sure of. One could go further on that.

Irvine moves slowly along the ridge between the two Steps. It is much narrower than he expected. He is reminded of the boards he and his friends used to place across the gap in the old canal footbridge near home. He almost puts his arms out for balance in imitation of his younger self above the dark and threatening water. There are moments when he is tempted to crawl, but occasionally he encounters the vague outline of a footprint that keeps him upright and resolved. He is labouring now, despite the gas, taking deeper and deeper breaths as he advances. When he climbs the Second Step, he thinks, there will be just over a tank left. Enough to get him to the top and back to the Step, surely. But after that? Well, Norton and Somervell made it down unmasked from almost that height. There is the question of time. Norton was in the Great Couloir at 1.00 p.m., and decided he had not enough daylight hours remaining for a summit push and safe return. He brings out his watch, and is surprised to see it is after 2.00 p.m. He looks up, and finds himself fewer than fifty yards from the Second Step. To get to the top, he will have to traverse outward on very exposed, snow-covered slabs to a small patch of ice and snow in the central split of rock. Once there, he will have a difficult fifteen-foot climb up the wall. He is thinking this over, getting ready to move to his right, when he sees someone in what looks like a hiking jacket and muffler sitting on the Step's far side, legs tucked beneath him, seemingly frozen in contemplation of the summit. There are no tanks on his back.

"Mallory," Irvine cries into his mask, and rips it off in frustration, tossing it away like a piece of old clothing he will not use again. "Mallory," into the breathed air of all the conviction he has ever possessed. The man's head turns slowly, so slowly that Irvine has time to imagine what those eyes must see while sweeping towards him, all God's grandeur spread out below. There is no other sign, but he has no choice. Mallory is in trouble. Any shreds of shame from this morning's discovery of the note are swept away. This is the vindication he has been seeking. Irvine knows Mallory has been to the top, but the world will not know it unless he brings him down. He sloughs off the tanks, checks his crampons, and begins the traverse. In less than thirty minutes he will meet his maker.

What could have been the most famous climb in history is over now, and hardly matters anymore. Mallory leaves the camp in starlight shortly after 5.00 a.m. and reaches the First Step two hours later. His experience in high places and his specific skills on rock and ice mean he can turn the Step in half the time it will later take Irvine. The subsequent trek along the mountain's spine is uneventful. He pays little attention to the oxygen regulator once he has set it at 1.5 litres per minute, which means he will not have enough to bring him down from the top. Noel's telephotos prove right. There are two towers to the Second Step with a large crack or gully between them. The snow patch provides a platform for ascent after a somewhat difficult traverse. When he arrives he studies the pitch. It is extremely jagged and cantilevered slightly outward, twenty feet high. He is up in fifteen minutes, and would be quicker but for the two heavy tanks. He peacefully studies the pyramid above him, higher now than anyone has been before. All sense of struggle with Everest has fallen away. No suitor caught in a dance of death, he is a figure in the panorama of his own superior vision. It is not the summit he holds in his mind's eye, but something more complex.

He decides to skirt the summit snowfield to the right, and then moves for the better part of an hour across a rocky plateau well down on the north side of the ridge and immediately above the Great Couloir. There is a small Third Step just three hundred feet from the top. The slabs on its right are very steep, but there is a narrow passage back onto the ridge proper. Here his chest begins to heave, and he fights for breath. He lets go the empty tanks in their aluminum frame over the ten thousand foot drop into Nepal. It has taken two hours from the Second Step to the ultimate arête. It is extremely narrow, and because his breath is coming now in short, sharp gasps, he drops to his knees and crawls the final few metres. It is noon, June 8, 1924. George Mallory is *ne plus ultra*.

To the south if he cared to look, are the jungles of Nepal, and to the east the tip of Kangchenjunga, some one thousand feet below. In a few hours the sun will set over Nanda Devi, which Odell, banished from Everest for a dozen years, will climb in near-middle age. But Mallory is concerned with only one direction. North into Tibet beyond the explorations of Younghusband, and so beyond the ken of any European. Out there somewhere is that peak whose lower shoulders he would stand on now if he were to walk out horizontally through the thin Tibetan air. It alone will tell him to descend, to go home, to start again his preparations for the climb. The minutes pass as he focuses on distant contours and lineations to no avail. Gradually, his gaze fixes on a line of jagged truth whose white proximity blinds his inner sight. *The mind has mountains.* He wheels on the tiny dais, his balance preserving him for the end, and looks down the Northeast Ridge. A diminutive black dot is silhouetted on the rocky terrace before the First Step, its movement barely perceptible against the darkness of the incline. "*Turn*," says Mallory, "*turn, turn, turn again.*" And begins his descent into silence.

Irvine struggles mightily on the traverse to the base of the second tower. It is the most difficult piece of climbing he has encountered in his very short career, and he is fortunate that the weather has held for him, and that the rock slabs he is crossing have next to no snow in their crevices. His face is more painful than ever, especially where the edges of the mask have rubbed it raw. He cannot get enough air, and regrets his impetuous disposal of the oxygen equipment, though he feels only one load now upon his broad shoulders. So he concentrates on the job at hand. To reach the snow patch and make contact with Mallory. If he cannot talk him down the wall, then he will have to climb up and get him. All thoughts of his own summit quest have long since vanished. Nothing remains but the less glorious yet vital role of disciple. Andrew Irvine is in love with what he has to do.

At the base of the pitch, he staggers a little, and looks up. The rocks are in the shadow, slick with ice. "Mallory," he cries again. "Mallory." No response, only the sharp edge of rock against the deepest blue he has ever known. He tries to strap his ice-axe at his waist, but fumbles with the belt. He lays the axe down in the snow and begins his climb, hand over hand. What he does is arduous because he is not versed in the practice, because he is very cold, and because his lungs feel as if they are in his throat and are ripped with every breath. But this is his deliverance, and he is equal to the task.

Halfway up he calls the name again. And a face appears above the boundary where the rocks meet a sky suddenly laced with cloud, a strange face he does not recognize at first. "George, George," Irvine calls excitedly, "Did you get there? Are you all right?" The face nods once, affirming one question or two, but it does not matter. It is the unmistakable gesture of the arm and hand sweeping out across the azure precipice that almost tears Irvine from the wall in shock. Mallory is telling him to go back, pushing at him through the air between them. The pressure is palpable, but Irvine, more certain than ever that Mallory is hurt and wants no sacrifice on his account, climbs on. When he is nearly there, Mallory leans over the edge and places his hands on Irvine's head, as if in benediction, but the result is fatal. Irvine resists the blessing of constraint and loses his hold. For a moment Mallory clasps his head inches from his own. Their eyes wide open to the love and horror. And then his body's weight pulls Irvine away from grace and into the void. Although he drops straight down and hits the snow patch with his feet, the momentum turns him abruptly sideways and into a projecting rock. The blood pours from his head as he reels from the tawny wall of Everest and tumbles into unrelenting space.

Mallory reaches out to the boy too late, and is inexorably pulled by the rent in the atmosphere over the rim of the tower toward the bright red pool below. He turns in mid-air and feels his cheeks carressed by every particle of haven and regret the rock-face can reflect. And lands beside the notched axe of Andrew Irvine, their blood mingling in frozen granules already blowing in the wind. For a long time he does not move. Except for his face, he is unhurt. But the damage spreads inside to stain the mountain and all his obsession with the crimson fact of Irvine's sacrifice and the dreadful blackness of self-loathing. A piece of the mountain that Irvine hit has broken off. He picks it up and puts it in his pocket. Then he takes the ice-axe by its head and pulls it from the snow. *Ah my dear,/ Fall, gall ourselves, and gash gold-vermilion.*

EIGHT

They are caught between what they never recognize as an inadequate devotion in themselves and a curbed sense of the holy space they have entered. I watch Mallory as he skips from rock to rock in a mountain stream in Bhutan. In his suit jacket, tie, shorts, and knee socks he carries England lightly on his shoulders, like a day-pack for lunch beside the Cam. The film jumps, and he is naked beside the water, the lower half of his body discreetly hidden by a boulder as he drinks and bathes himself, laughing at someone or something we do not see. It cannot have been staged. Too much baggage strewn around, the coolies threatening from the ragged edges of the frame, Captain Noel with the heavy camera sweating in the jungle above. Nonetheless it is a pose: the sahib at play a few weeks before the final, deadly movements in the game.

Compare the relaxed, secular strength of Mallory's frame with the faithful body of the Tibetan pilgrim who measures his own length on the ground for two hundred miles towards Everest, putting his hands together at his forehead, bowing, kneeling, and lying prostrate in devout repetition for forty times the height of the mountain. Of course, the pilgrim will never actually climb Chomolungma, never feel the bite of her legendary phantom guard dogs above the North Col, or question the tenets of his desire as their talons rip away his certainties at 28,000 feet to expose the mortal flesh beneath. This is where the comparison breaks down.

126

The pilgrim spurns the fugitive nature of his earthly existence to achieve nirvana, while the integrity of Mallory's crusade depends upon the ascent of Everest in order (Noel's words) *to touch the very doors of heaven.*

Everything about the British Film Institute is neat and efficient, or seems to be. A monied, modern building in Central London that bears no resemblance to the relative sidestreet poverty of the Alpine Club. I sign in at the desk, watched by two women in blue uniforms. After one of them makes a phone call, I am admitted to the inner sanctum and descend to a very different kind of basement. But there is no Mr. Peters to accompany me, and I wander unsupervised through a labyrinth of halls that open on doors to rooms where expensive equipment and reels of presumably valuable film lie untended. It is amazing what is surrendered to a signature. Irvine's ice-axe is here somewhere for the taking.

The guardian dog is a friendly technician who takes me to a cubicle where five canisters of Noel's cinematic production await. I am given a thirty-second course in how to load a reel and operate the controls of the tiny screen, and he departs. A child of the movies and more recently of home video, I have come to meet Mallory's image. Like that storied indigene who believes the picture of a man captures his soul.

It will be twenty-five years before the Chinese colonize Tibet. It is a country the English will never understand or control. The all-powerful expedition requires a pass from the Dalai Lama in Llasa: *It is known that a group of Sahibs wish to climb our sacred Chomolungma. You shall provide for them and watch over them.* But a pass is a mere formality in this country of children who live in hovels, never wash, and keep toe-nail parings to ward off misadventure (the climber practises but never admits to superstition). If you laugh a lot and keep talking, as General Bruce did in '22, you can communicate with them. They are essentially a *happy* people, and their babies are *quaint little beings.* What does Noel say to them through the interpreter whose name was Karma? "Tibetans, please"? And they just smile and smile, having no family troubles or daily struggles to survive, economically and psychologically, those nail clippings absorbing all of life's complexities with crescent care. Until the Rongbuk Monastery.

Mallory, Norton, and Irvine watch the temple dancers across the monastery's inner square. They are masked and wear aprons made from human bones. The dance of death is performed to show how the spirits of good and evil will be met in the afterworld.

"It's quite a show," says Irvine. It is his first visit to the monastery.

"Yes, and it's never quite the same, is it George?"

Mallory takes a moment to reply, and then does not answer Norton's question. "How thin the line is for them between life and death. The one is just a pathway to the other. Chomolungma is not a distant peak to be overcome, but the mother goddess among them now."

Norton looks at him. George is the expedition philosopher, so anything he says along such lines is bound to have merit. Although Norton is the climbing leader, he will defer in almost every way to Mallory's views, as long as there are no surprises, nothing from the blind side. Indeed, it is when Norton *is* blind, his sight taken by the snow, that he will assume his full rank and lead his bloodied lieutenant from the field of conquest.

"Do they live here all the time? The monks, I mean."

"Yes. But then you must remember that time does not really exist for them." Mallory is patient with Irvine, Norton notes, instructing him carefully and in simple terms as he will later on the mountain. "This monastery is a kind of penance for them before they enter paradise. If they seem concerned with death, it is only because life concerns them very little. If you told them what we are doing, they would understand, but it would mean nothing to them."

"What about the Lama?"

"Oh, he is a wise man who must have climbed some mountains of his own to get where he is. I think he is intrigued by our attempt to reach the top because he does not believe it is possible.

128

He has already told us that the gods of the Lamas will deny us the object of our search."

"Will they?" Norton smiles. Young Irvine is so direct. If he were in command, they would simply assault the north face.

"I honestly don't know, Sandy. I'm inclined to believe that Everest will yield to our best efforts. But I thought that in '22 as well. Seven men died as a result."

Now Norton is surprised. Apart from their mutual and natural agreement in London that no lives must be lost on this expedition, Mallory has never indicated any strong concern about the accident, despite the criticism from some old Alpine Club members who don't know the Himalayas (Norton is not aware of his *cri de coeur* to Geoffrey Young). "Come, George, that was not your fault. None of us thought that snow could shift the way it did."

Norton is disturbed by Mallory's response, though he has not read Hopkins nor is likely to. *"'Death,' said I, 'what do you here/At this Spring season of the year?'/'I mark the flowers ere the prime/Which I may tell at Autumn time'..../And the flowers that he had tied/As I mark'd not always died/Sooner than their mates; and yet/Their fall was fuller of regret:"*

This dance is over. The masks are doffed and replaced by others, together with tight-fitting clothes that have the figures of skeletons painted on them. "The cemetery ghoul dance," says Mallory. "That pile of scarves represents the mortal clay."

Irvine is slightly repulsed by the performance. Somehow the heap of coloured cloth troubles him more than would an actual body. A slight wind in the courtyard flutters the scarves, though the dancers take pains to avoid them. The carved features of the masks seem to ripple with movement, and are terrible in their display. Thank God, he thinks, there are no monasteries on Everest itself. In anticipation of the monkless climb, he licks his dry lips, feeling the heat on his extended tongue that will soon be wet with absolution's blood. And laughs at the Tibetans who appear to mimic him, not knowing that the gesture here is a polite form of greeting, a humbling of the self because the invitation is to cut off what may possibly offend.

I lipread some of this frame by frame, and rely on Noel's subtitles for the overall expression of attitude (*the happiest of all is a beggar in the market; the pretty Tibetan women are always smiling and jolly*). The rest I must possibly imagine, though the quotation from Hopkins is in Mallory's journal. When Noel's camera captures the climbers retiring for the night to their tiny cells, the iron doors clang without sound, and the aperture closes down to black. I am left peering through the bars at sleeping forms that twitch to the dance's rhythm like puppets in a dark belay.

Irvine lies inert at Mallory's feet, while the others shuffle slowly around them, roped together, bits of equipment hanging from their torsos, their leather and rubber masks in place, the tubes like growths from their mouths snaking back to the twin tanks of English air. The Lama blesses them from afar, the prayer wheels turning a thousand times, the scarves now blowing in a wind of white flowers that rise to cover the climbers in a panoply of petals. And then not petals but bits of scripted paper that envelop them, resting finally on their flaking lips and foreheads and escaping strands of greasy hair before they disappear beneath this weight of words, the ones they have themselves written and have yet to write in order to explain their fate.

We are nature's children. When we die she holds us to her bosom. But that is too general for the specific endeavour to be celebrated here. Thus, *Who would ask to lie in any other place than beneath a bed of virgin snow or artless pile of rock?* And then Odell emerges from the burial mound to spread six blankets out in the form of a cross, the official sign that all hope is gone, followed by Norton who lays three others side by side that signal *Abandon hope. Descend without delay.* Such platitudes do not suffice, and the writers know this. Some explanation must be offered for death and failure (and Mallory's mad betrayal of them all). Everest becomes animate now, not just another piece of rock to assault and vanquish: *How pitiless and scornful of human endeavour this mountain was.* But neither is that enough because the mountain personified still should not defeat the pursuit of English ideals. More is necessary here to haunt the imaginations of readers so they will search between the lines uneasily for answers that will never come, while Norton and Young manipulate the silence: *In the end we embraced a cause beyond our ken. These people of a simple faith* [who put on quite a show] *believe that Everest lives and is protected by spirits.*

Noel's final shot is of the entire north face of Everest bathed in sunlight and then claimed by shadow from the base to the summit pyramid, the plume of snow streaming from the awful mouths of the demon dogs or even from the disdainful lips of the Mother Goddess herself.

There is no camera any more. Only a dream so clear. *When I awake in the tent there is a man beside me. For some reason I don't question the tent, the extreme cold, the wind that is howling outside. It is the man who holds me. The face is familiar. It is a face from books. 'You're Mallory,' I say.*

"Yes. And you are the story-teller."

"No, that was Davies. I just listened to him."

"You conjured up Davies to serve your ends."

"Wait a minute. I didn't know he would be waiting in Wales. I went there simply to see where you had climbed when you were young. I chose the Llanberis Lodge purely by chance. He was in the garden. That's when everything took off."

"In the direction you wanted it to go."

"It's not that easy. And the control you suggest certainly isn't there. When I started I was trying to deal with the dreams I was having about you. So I read a lot about you. Books, your letters, what your fellow climbers said."

"Then what?"

"Then that official story about your death started to unravel. It was all so perfect, so pure. Even though you died on Everest, there were no flaws."

"So you went looking for flaws. The ironic residue of your world."

"Not exactly. But I began to think about other possibilities. And part of it was in response to the various searches for bits of evidence that would prove you made it to the top, or find your body, or Irvine's, in some position that would at least indicate what had happened to you."

"Like finding Icarus, you said."

"Yes. Only someone else came up with that metaphor first. I just took it a little further.

"And the other possibilities?"

"Everything about you was so wrapped up in the heroic figure myth. Galahad after the Grail. Your pure white chivalrous manhood. Part of it attracts me. I've read enough of the poems you liked to read, for one thing. But what stunned me was the insistence of Geoffrey Young and the others who loved you that the world and values you knew before the War were still intact. All that insanity should have blown them away. It did blow them away, along with Wilfred Owen who put the lie to the glory of sacrifice. What was your death compared to the deaths of the millions in the trenches? Whatever your individual courage and sense of purpose, I thought it was crazy to canonize you for a whole nation or for the English-speaking world. Anything I came up with couldn't be any crazier than that."

"I might have done the same thing, you know."

"What do you mean?"

"If I had written Geoffrey's obituary. If he had been younger and hadn't lost his leg, and had disappeared on Everest. You have to understand what it meant to climb together in those days. Before the War we questioned a lot of things, but never the code that we adhered to in the mountains. When I was in France, it sometimes was the only thing between me and the chaos, the insanity as you say. Afterwards, so many reacted with carelessness and abandon. They took terrible chances, and simply didn't care anymore. We did care. We cared passionately about how we climbed, and what seemed like risk to others was really measured common sense given the ground we trod."

"But you weren't private individuals. You represented something to people."

"Inspiration, perhaps?"

"Yes, inspiration. But like that in the charge of the Light Brigade, at least as Tennyson presents it. Though I'd like to read some irony in that poem."

"There was no irony."

"Just messy death, covered up by fine words. The myth of history had you and Irvine stepping painlessly into a veil of clouds so that the myth-readers wouldn't dwell on your screams as you fell, or on your ravings as you froze to death on a mountain-side that was far too big for you. Bigger in ways than your precious Empire had ever been."

"And what of you? What have you and Davies done, and that actress you went to see?"

"Told another story."

"But what kind of story? You and Davies say that I didn't die on that last climb. That Sandy fell, and they found me out of my head. So Teddy Norton, a brilliant climber and leader of men but without much imagination, concocted a conspiracy virtually by himself and then brought Geoffrey Young along. Geoffrey, who was honest to a fault and detested hypocrisy."

"No. You see, Norton didn't construct the conspiracy by himself. None of you were alone on Everest. You took all the baggage of English history and culture, or what you thought were English history and culture, with you. When you said you had killed Irvine, you isolated yourself from that past and from your own, original membership in it. You had to be dealt with accordingly. You were meant to reach the summit without any problem, or to die. There was no in between allowed. Given this, what they proposed to do--and did, according to Davies--was easy compared to any alternative."

"But doesn't he create another myth? Mallory, or Jones as I am renamed, retires into the mystery of silence, and then is rescued by a boy who is just another version of himself. No one knows about this counter-myth until you come along and rescue it from oblivion."

"Maybe it's a myth, or counter-myth. First of all, it's a story. And I emphasize that. But Davies was very real to me in that garden in Llanberis, and very convincing."

133

"Wasn't he telling you what you were prepared to hear. And to believe? Others will want to believe it too."

"Listen, if I ever write this up, there will be hell to pay. That brotherhood to which you belonged is still flourishing. They can dismiss you as just a figment of my imagination, a face from books. But Davies is something else. There are those in Llanberis who knew him. Thomas at the Llanberis Lodge for one. I don't know what's happened to his papers. Maybe they've been thrown out. Maybe not."

"But you do know you've no proof of anything, even if they are still there. Donald's letters and Jones's note to him confirm nothing at all."

"You're right. Maybe there's an original text. Maybe not. And that tale, if it exists, is simply open to interpretation. Davies can't be questioned anymore. Knowing him, I think he would have stuck to his guns whatever pressure he had to bear. But doesn't that connect him to Norton, Young, and Odell, none of whom are alive either? Their texts remain, and readers do with them what they have to. There's absolutely no proof as to your death on Everest, just speculation, and that's all there ever will be."

"What was that actress's name?"

"Madeleine Carroll."

"Yes. Why did you have to go to see her? Why bring Ruth into it after all these years?"

"For one thing, whatever I've read on you contains only edited versions of her. She was your beautiful, suffering helpmate according to your biographers. The only time she's quoted is when she's writing to you in Tibet. No woman has written about you, or her. No, that's not quite true. There was one who co-wrote a book on the search for clues of what happened to you and Irvine. But, for me, it's essentially a climber's book with some consideration of your cultural and sexual affiliations. Your marriage is scrutinized, but Ruth's voice is circumscribed by whatever it is you're doing at the time. Certainly there's never any mention about what happened to her after 1924. What kind of a life could she have had anyway, without you, I mean? And, yes, I am being ironic."

"But for someone to suggest that I could have been alive all those years without her knowing."

"In pure story terms, I'd say it freed her, at least to some extent. She became an Everest widow. Otherwise, she might have cared for you for the rest of your life, or hers, nursemaid to a patient who would have continually reminded her of the past or else have woken up one day and wreaked havoc with the myth she had helped sustain. That leaves aside any question of her possible involvement in Norton and Young's plan. But maybe one of the important points here is that nothing in any of these stories about you, Davies' and my own included, is purely personal. There's a kind of collective need to pursue myth and to reshape or rewrite it in one form or another. Others dream of you, or of someone like you, all the time, I'm sure."

"So for you, that man Donat was right? 'Sticks in the sand,' wasn't it?"

"Yes. Though that only complicates everything about you."

"I should think it would greatly simplify things. It does away with responsibilty, for one thing. You, or Davies, tell a story about me. It doesn't matter whether it's true or not. You are supposedly part of some larger need."

"Davies told me that something is true according to those who need to believe it is true. Does it matter whether the tale of you and Irvine disappearing on Everest can be proved or not? I mean in a final sense? It's made up of truths that have to do with who you were, what you tried to do, and the impact on those who watched and waited. In the end what you tried to do was greater than what you did. Who you were was smaller than the figure you had become. I think Norton and Young knew that. Whether you actually disappeared on the mountain or were brought back to Llanberis, they knew that. You were a climber in 1924. If you later wrote those journals that Davies gave me to read, you were coming to terms with something more than climbing. If Davies wrote them, he was, in his way, trying to make you bigger than the figure you had become. You're dead now. That's the only certainty."

"What will you do with all this?"

"I don't know. I do know that my thoughts and feelings about you are complex. They always have been. I dream about you. I read about you. I write about you. Is there any difference? I could change all the names and dates. Only Everest would stay the same. But people would see through that. The nicety of the deflected narrative. Why not call you Jones from the beginning, for example, and give you another name when you come back to North Wales? Wouldn't that do away with the dependence on truth through naming? Or would it keep the comfortable distance intact, for most people, between fiction and fact? But I didn't give Nye Davies a psuedonym, and I could have done that. What I will have to do is call any book I write about you a novel. Someone said, perhaps an Italian from the thirteenth century, that we must consider not what books say, but what they mean.

"I can't promise to leave you alone."

"No, I don't imagine you can."

At the base of the west side of the Second Step, 700 vertical feet from the summit, there is an ice cave among the boulders. It is large enough for several people.

He is there in front of me, his form outlined against the whiteness of the ridge extending beyond us in the dark. We move along the arête between the Steps into a wind without cease. It bites through my sweaters and anorak and the wool pants I wear with the corduroy ones beneath. The weight of the tanks on my back is incredible, and I gag on the rubber tube in my mouth with every heaving breath I take. There is a pounding in my head, and I feel as if I will die of thirst if I do not slip into the black vacuity on either side. His pace is relentless, though the rope between us does not grow taut. I have little climbing experience, but a laughing Welsh voice offers encouragement. "That's it boyo. The ice is not so bad, is it? He's thinking of himself, not you, so stick close, and watch his feet."

I fear the Second Step we are approaching, and am about to pull on the rope, to tell him he should go on alone, when suddenly he stops and motions me to join him. There is still the traverse out along the face, but the void is now a benefit as I focus on the steep slope that curves to the tiny platform in the severed rock. This is the cold heaven of balance I have found and the adumbration of ascent. Even so, I stumble at the cave's entrance and crawl on my knees into the cleft. I hear the clang of metal on rock as the tanks are ripped away and the tube slides out across my teeth. I suck the remnants of my breath, but the weight behind is even heavier until a hand removes it, as I stand in the enclosed space to find the others waiting there.

Davies is in his chair, the blanket across his knees; Donald in his airman's uniform, a leather flying helmet in his hands; and Madeleine Carroll in her white linen suit, on the table beside her the pictures of herself like holographs carved from ice. Mallory hands me a knapsack that I realize holds the box of letters and his journal typescript he has taken from my back.

"This is what they are looking for."

"Yes," I reply. "What do you want me to do with them?"

He shrugs, but does not turn away. The others gaze silently. And I understand it is entirely up to me. At head level there is a crooked fissure in the rock like a mouth about to open or close. I push the package in until just memory remains. When I turn to seek assurance from their eyes, they are memory too.

Before I go home I drive to Llanberis once again, this time up the motorway from London. It is a Thursday afternoon in mid-May when I arrive, and the tourists are out in force. Thomas greets me at the Lodge and tells me he can put me up for only a night because a party of executives on an outward bound course is coming from Manchester for the weekend.

"I've cleaned out his room," he tells me. "Gave some things to the Sally Ann, and tossed the rest. But these I kept for you." He hands me the box wrapped round with the yellow band.

"Thanks," I say. "Will you have a drink with me later?"

"Of course. We'll raise a glass to him."

It takes me the better part of an hour to walk up to the Pass, and another thirty or forty minutes to reach the foot of Graig Dhu. The waters of Llyn Idwal reflect the changing shadows of the cliff and the deep blue of the spring sky that is not blue at all. I build my fire of sticks and words, and watch the west wind blow a plume of smoke into the light.